T0128313

THE ARTIFACT

PREVIOUS BOOKS BY ALAN REFKIN

FICTION

Matt Moretti and Han Li Series

The Archivist
The Abductions
The Payback

Mauro Bruno Detective Series

The Patriarch
The Scion

NONFICTION

The Wild, Wild East: Lessons for Success in Business in Contemporary Capitalist China
Alan Refkin and Daniel Borgia, PhD

Doing the China Tango: How to Dance around Common Pitfalls in Chinese Business Relationships
Alan Refkin and Scott Cray

Conducting Business in the Land of the Dragon: What Every Businessperson Needs to Know about China
Alan Refkin and Scott Cray

Piercing the Great Wall of Corporate China: How to Perform Forensic Due Diligence on Chinese Companies
Alan Refkin and David Dodge

THE ARTIFACT

A MAURO BRUNO DETECTIVE SERIES THRILLER

ALAN REFKIN

THE ARTIFACT
A MAURO BRUNO DETECTIVE SERIES THRILLER

This is a work of fiction. All the characters, names, incidents, organizations, and dialogue in this novel are either the products of the author's imagination or are used fictitiously.

iUniverse books may be ordered through booksellers or by contacting:

iUniverse
1663 Liberty Drive
Bloomington, IN 47403
www.iuniverse.com
1-800-Authors (1-800-288-4677)

ISBN: 978-1-6632-0074-7 (sc)
ISBN: 978-1-6632-0075-4 (e)

Library of Congress Control Number: 2020908840

Print information available on the last page.

iUniverse rev. date: 06/11/2020

To my wife, Kerry
To Shirley Goodburn

CHAPTER 1

PAOLO NICCHI WAS attempting to elude Armanno Rotolo with every ounce of speed he could order his nonmuscular legs to generate. Failure wasn't an option because just moments ago, as Nicchi was speaking with a reporter, Rotolo had come out of nowhere and shot the reporter in the face at point-blank range with a silenced handgun. Standing next to Rotolo had been Antonio Conti. The billionaire founder, chairman, and CEO of Conti Petroleum was one of the wealthiest and most respected businessmen in Italy.

Nicchi had never seen someone killed before and had frozen in stark terror as he watched the man's body collapse to the ground, as if a puppeteer had suddenly cut the strings to his creation. Not questioning why Rotolo didn't turn and shoot him while he stood looking at the body with his mouth hanging open, Nicchi took off as fast as he could, determined that only a heart attack would slow him down. That he would suffer a myocardial infarction was a distinct possibility because the fifty-eight-year-old, five-foot-five, 260-pound light-skinned Italian was what some might refer to as a marshmallow—soft and weak.

Earlier, he'd been enjoying a Peroni beer with the newspaper reporter at a tavern in Taranto, a coastal Italian city of two hundred thousand on the Ionian Sea. Although Nicchi lived in Monopoli, on the opposite coast of the heel of the Italian boot, the Adriatic Sea side of Apulia, he was only forty miles from home. Sitting next to the reporter in a booth, he had given the man an eight-by-eleven manila folder that he said contained journalistic dynamite—a fact the reporter had confirmed upon seeing the contents: four photos that proved Antonio Conti was a terrorist. Unfortunately, the billionaire had somehow learned about the meeting, which was why Nicchi was now literally running for his life.

Nicchi veered to his right and went down an alley, hoping a change in direction would allow him to escape the killer. As his breathing became increasingly ragged, and his brain ordered his body to take in great gulps of air to try to get more oxygen into his lungs, he became fatigued, and his pace decreased to little more than a fast walk. If he had his phone, he could call the police. But he'd dropped it outside the tavern—the result of totally freaking out when he saw the reporter's face explode.

He'd picked this reporter because Nicchi's research had shown that the man wasn't afraid to take anyone on, having written articles on corrupt politicians and scams orchestrated by several local businesses. He'd gotten the reporter's phone number from the paper's web page and called and left a message. An hour later, the reporter had returned his call, but he was in Naples at the time, so the earliest he could meet was the following day at midnight. He suggested a local tavern that was in a secluded location and open until 2:00 a.m.

The meeting had gone exceptionally well, with the reporter asking a great many questions. They'd spoken until the tavern closed, after which they'd continued their discussion outside. They'd been outside for less than thirty seconds when the killer and Conti approached. No words were exchanged. After a nod from Conti, Rotolo had simply raised his gun and killed the reporter.

Nicchi's woefully unathletic legs began to cramp because of a buildup of lactic acid. He became light-headed and was on the verge of passing out, his body unable to get the oxygen it needed. The result was an emergency cease-and-desist signal sent by his brain to his legs to stop all movement. He collapsed knees first to the ground and crawled out of the street to the adjacent sidewalk, eventually leaning his back against the wall of a commercial building while he tried to regain his strength.

A minute later, Rotolo and Conti approached. While Rotolo kept his gun aimed at the exhausted geologist, Conti crouched down so that he was eye level with his recreant employee. In his hands he was holding Nicchi's cell phone and the folder that he had given to the reporter.

"Do you know what I value the most, Paolo?" Conti asked.

Nicchi shook his head no.

"Loyalty. I let you into my tribe, so to speak, and you repay this kindness by putting a dagger in my back. Fortunately, you called the reporter while standing near my company cell tower, which records every conversation passing through it. Otherwise, I wouldn't have known about your meeting," Conti said, the disdain apparent in his voice.

"Perhaps—"

Conti cut him off with an imperious wave of his hand. "Perhaps I should forget about this treachery? Not ever. You made your choice."

Nicchi stared at the ground in front of him.

"Let's go somewhere private," Conti said. Standing up, he whispered something to his assassin.

In response, Rotolo bent down and punched Nicchi in the jaw, rendering him unconscious. He then hoisted the hefty geologist over his shoulders in a fireman's carry and followed his boss toward the wharf. It took twelve minutes to get to the Airbus AS365 Dauphin helicopter that was waiting for them in an empty parking lot. Once Nicchi was lying on his back on the steel deck and Conti had climbed aboard, Rotolo told the pilot to take off.

Conti and Rotolo, who sat side by side, were a contrast in both appearance and background. Conti was forty-one years old, five feet, seven inches tall, weighed 171 pounds, and had thick black hair that he kept short enough so that it didn't have to be combed. He had a beak-like nose, medium brown skin, and black eyes that resembled round opals floating in a pool of white. Overall, he looked more Middle Eastern than Italian. The reason for this seeming contradiction was that Antonio Conti's birth name was Ammar Nadeem. The son of al-Qaeda terrorist parents who were killed in a NATO airstrike in Iraq, he had been orphaned at the age of two and had been taken in by Sargon Zebari, the leader of al-Qaeda, who became his adoptive father.

Zebari, a man with neither compassion nor remorse, had not been the least bit altruistic in bringing Nadeem to live with him. Rather, he had been formulating a plan that required someone of a young age who could be ideologically indoctrinated and would obey his orders now and in the future without hesitation—even at the cost of his own life.

Armanno Rotolo, in contrast to his boss, was six feet, three inches in height and appeared to have not an ounce of fat on his 190-pound chiseled body. Conti's enforcer was someone many women would refer to as a hunk. He had light brown skin, a neatly trimmed black beard, wide-set eyes that were black and expressionless, and a Roman nose that had a slight downward bend from the bridge. His midfade haircut was spiky on the top and decreased in length as it went down the sides of his head until it was little more than stubble. The absence of gray in his jet-black hair made him look five years younger than his thirty-five years. Rotolo was also a member of al-Qaeda and had been sent by Zebari, when Conti got older, to work with and protect him.

"Wake him up," Conti said, turning to his enforcer.

Rotolo got out of his seat, which was to the left of Conti, and lifted Nicchi off the deck. He then lightly slapped the side of the geologist's face until he regained consciousness.

"Where are we going?" Nicchi asked, still groggy as he looked around him.

"We're going back to the rig."

Conti then directed Rotolo, who had one hand on each of the geologist's arms to steady him, to put Nicchi into the seat next to him.

"Who are you, and what are you after? Smuggling arms and men into Italy are acts of terrorism. Are you a terrorist?" Nicchi asked, apparently setting aside his fear because he knew he had no control over his fate. He looked Conti straight in the eye.

"I'm a servant of Allah."

Nicchi, with a look of bewilderment, stared hard at him. "Everyone in Italy knows your story of being kidnapped as a child and growing up in an Italian orphanage. When did you convert to Islam?"

"I'm Muslim by birth and heritage. I was born in Iraq, which I consider my homeland. I can see you're confused, so let me tell you a story, since we have some time till we get to where we're going." Conti went on to relate how he had been orphaned at two and for the next five years had received religious schooling and language training until he could speak the Italian dialect of the Apulia region perfectly. Once his education was complete, he had been smuggled into Italy and abandoned outside a police station in Monopoli.

"Why Monopoli?" Nicchi interrupted.

"Because it's a sparsely populated fishing village that, even now, doesn't have the coastal security of larger towns and cities."

Conti then continued, explaining that he had given a carefully crafted story of being kidnapped and taken from city to city until he was eventually sold to someone.

"And how did you get your name?"

"I told the police that I had been kidnapped when I was much younger and therefore didn't remember my last name. However, I did recall that my first name was Antonio. It didn't seem unreasonable to forget my surname." He then recalled how the police checked and double-checked the surrounding towns and cities, then the entire country, for any record of the disappearance of a boy his age named Antonio. But they obviously found none since the kidnapping was a hoax. The court subsequently placed him in an orphanage, where he was to stay until someone came forward with proof of parentage. Eventually, he was adopted by a local family.

"So that's how you got your last name. You were lucky that someone adopted you."

"Lucky? Luck had nothing to do with it. My adoptive father put together an ingenious plan that was perfectly executed. Whether I was adopted or not, the result would have been the same. My ascendance in the business community and future wealth were orchestrated. For example, it was determined that I should be a petroleum engineer, and thanks to anonymous scholarships my schools received, that occurred. When it was time for me to get a job, my adoptive father used his influential contacts to get me a position in an Italian petroleum company where, thanks to the business I was fed, I became the biggest rainmaker and deal saver. As a result, I not only gained valuable industry experience but also rapidly ascended the corporate ladder—as planned."

"And Conti Petroleum?"

"The result of a Swiss financial firm backing me in the buyout of the company for which I worked. Once I became the chairman and chief executive officer, the company's name was changed."

"Funded by al-Qaeda, I'm sure."

"Guilty as charged."

"One minute," the pilot said over the intercom.

"And you use your profits to fund terrorism throughout Italy."

"Throughout the world. With ten oil platforms in the Adriatic Sea and your expertise in finding natural gas deposits in the tracts I've leased, and those I intend to lease, I expect to more than double the hundreds of millions in earnings that I currently generate."

"We're at the coordinates," the pilot said over the intercom.

"Make your height 125 feet," Rotolo said in his deep voice into the mic of the headset he was wearing.

The pilot did as he was told, pulling his craft up slightly. Conti nodded.

Without a word, Rotolo picked Nicchi up off his seat with one hand and slid open the helicopter door with the other.

In the blink of an eye, the geologist was tossed out the opening and into blackness outside. With a fall of over twelve stories, he impacted the water at sixty miles per hour. Statistically, his chances of survival from that height were approximately 10 percent—odds he didn't beat.

Once Nicchi was on his way into the Ionian Sea, Rotolo told the pilot to quickly descend and use the helicopter's powerful searchlight to find his body before the rotund corpse was swept away in the choppy seas or sank beneath the surface. It took five minutes to find the body, which was facedown in the water, rising and falling with the undulating waves. While the pilot held the aircraft steady, Rotolo swung out the overhead hoist, secured himself to a nylon harness attached to a steel cable, and lowered himself to the surface of the water. It took several attempts, with the pilot constantly adjusting for the movement of the body in the choppy seas, before Rotolo was able to grab hold of the body. Once Rotolo was back on board, Conti directed the pilot to fly to the hospital in Monopoli, which was the nearest town to his company's southernmost oil rig.

As the helicopter turned toward shore, Rotolo called the medical facility from his sat phone and informed them that he was en route from the oil rig with a worker who'd slipped and fallen from the platform's twelve-story derrick. As a result, when the Dauphin set down, a doctor and three nurses were waiting beside the landing pad with a gurney. Dashing on board the aircraft, the doctor went through the motion of listening for a heartbeat with his stethoscope. However, one look at Nicchi's pallor and his rolled-back eyes told the physician that this person's next examination would be performed by the coroner.

It was 6:00 a.m. when the Airbus AS365 Dauphin landed on the helipad of the Conti Petroleum oil platform, which was anchored to the floor of the Adriatic Sea seven miles off the coast of the Italian city of Monopoli. Conti went directly to his office-apartment, followed by Rotolo. Opening the folder that Nicchi had given the reporter, he looked at the first of three photos. It revealed a dozen scruffy men getting off two inflatable rafts, the Conti Petroleum logo clearly visible on the side of a derrick in the background. Each of the men was carrying a weapon, and they didn't look like a group that intended to queue for customs and immigration and present their passports. From a close look at the photo, it was obvious that Nicchi had taken the shot from his cell phone while in the smoking section on the main deck, an area that was not readily visible from either the helipad or the platform's floating dock.

The second photo showed crates piled on the helipad, their contents stamped in English on the crates' sides— assault rifles, handguns, and hand grenades—and the Conti Petroleum helicopter in the background. The third photograph was the most incriminating for Conti since it showed him hefting a crate of Colt M4 carbines onto his corporate helicopter. Conti grouped the photos together and fed them into the shredder beside his desk.

"Make sure you change the helicopter logs to reflect that Nicchi arrived on the platform just before midnight," Conti said, returning his attention to Rotolo, "and document that we called and asked him to return to the rig so that he could explain to us his report on undersea gas deposits prior to a 7:00 a.m. investor call."

"I'll make the changes now. But we have another problem," Rotolo said, unbuttoning the top of his shirt and pointing to his bare neck. Absent was the chain he always wore, which held a three-by-three-inch piece of silver punctuated with five rows of unevenly spaced holes. Conti, Zebari, and one other individual also had one.

"Where did you lose it?"

"While searching Nicchi's residence. I was in a hurry, and I must have caught it on something. I didn't notice that it was missing until I returned to my vehicle. By then it was too late to return and search for it because his neighbor had walked outside and was working in the yard. I left before he saw me."

"Use mine to make a paper copy until we can have a replacement made."

"Has the sheik arrived in Iran?" Rotolo asked. Although Zebari wasn't technically a sheik, he and Rotolo often referred to him as such as a sign of respect.

"I was just about to see," Conti said, booting up his computer and looking for an email from an oil and gas tooling company executive, which was the cover Zebari preferred to use. He found it and clicked on the print icon on his screen.

Conti removed the square from the silver box chain around his neck, pulled the page from the printer, and laid the silver pendant over the email's text so that the upper left hole was centered over the first exclamation mark. He then began to copy the letters that were under each hole. When he ran out of holes, he found the next exclamation mark and repeated the process. Six placements later, he had his message.

"The sheik is in Tehran and has the flower," Conti said, using the code word that he and Zebari had devised for the dirty bomb, effectively a radiological dispersal device used against civilians. Rather than kill, it was meant to instill fear and panic and cause significant economic damage due to the enormous time and expense it would take to clean up the affected area.

"Praise be to Allah. May he guide us in killing the infidels to avenge more than a millennium of injustice that the West has inflicted on our brothers. Inshallah," Rotolo said with enthusiasm.

"Yes, if Allah wills it," Conti repeated.

CHAPTER 2

T HE FIRM WAS called BD&D Investigations and was named after Mauro Bruno, Elia Donati, and Lisette Donais. Bruno formerly had been a chief inspector with the Italian state police in Venice, and Donati had held the same rank in Milan. Donais had previously been an investigator for a law firm in Paris. They'd come together under adverse circumstances when Bruno and Donati were framed for murder by the scion of a billionaire who believed they had driven his father to commit suicide by bringing his family's criminal past to light. Working together, and evading numerous attempts on their lives, the three had been able to clear their names and bring their accuser to justice. Afterward, as they were about to return to their previous employment, each had realized that the synergy and camaraderie between them had become far too great to abandon. As a result, BD&D Investigations was born. It had two offices—one in Milan and the other in Paris, with the latter housed in Donais's apartment.

The Milan office was a 2,800-square-foot four-bedroom apartment located a few steps from the Duomo. It was on the second floor of a white five-story historic building in the Corso Di Porta Romana neighborhood of Milan. The interior was painted entirely in white and had antique stressed wood flooring throughout. The entrance hall led to a large room that offered a magnificent view of a private garden and courtyard, its mature trees soaring past the apartment's windows. Bruno, Donati, and Donais used this room as their workspace.

BD&D's office furnishings were spartan, consisting of a rectangular conference table surrounded by eight black Herman Miller Aeron mesh-back chairs. Because of the lack of space, the conference table functioned as a communal desk. A seventy-inch TV dominated the office wall opposite the windows. To the left of the work area was a kitchen, which adjoined a laundry room, utility room, and bathroom. Each of the partners had a private bedroom and bath. The fourth bedroom, which was the largest, was used for storage and housed the office printer, copier, and server. The bedrooms were to the right as one entered the apartment.

The three partners had started their investigative service believing that they'd receive referrals from Donais's former employer, the state police, other government agencies they'd interacted with over the years, and law firms that were familiar with their investigative expertise. All had agreed that after setting up their office, they'd cast their lines in the water and see if their expectations became reality. Therefore, what occurred was totally unexpected.

Donais was hanging a picture on the wall when Dante Acardi, deputy commissioner of the Italian state police, opened their office door and entered unannounced. The trim, five-foot-eight sexagenarian, with short gray hair parted to the right and light brown eyes, was carrying a black leather briefcase in his right hand and was accompanied by a five-foot-four middle-aged woman. From a distance the black hair made her appear younger than she was, but as she approached the investigators, each noticed the hands, arms, and wrinkled skin of someone in her midfifties. The anguish on her face gave the impression that she'd recently experienced a trauma, which they later learned she had. Donais, with no idea who'd barged into their office, eased her hand into her right jacket pocket, where she kept a small handgun.

"Good morning," Acardi said in a baritone voice.

"It's all right, Lisette," Bruno said, apparently noticing the movement of her hand. He and Donati stepped forward to greet their former boss.

Donais removed her hand from her jacket pocket and joined them.

"Let me introduce our partner, Lisette Donais," Bruno said.

"The rose between two thorns," Acardi replied, stepping forward and giving her a light kiss on both cheeks. He then introduced the woman he was with as Lia Nicchi.

"How did you get into the building?" Bruno asked.

Reaching into his jacket pocket, Acardi removed and displayed his credentials. That was how.

"Can I get either of you an espresso? A water?" Bruno asked. When both declined, he directed them to the conference table.

Bruno, a forty-nine-year-old former chief inspector from Venice, sat at the head of the table, with Donati to his right and Donais to his left. Bruno wore his uniform of a dark blue suit, white shirt, and light blue tie, with Donati's daily attire virtually the same except for his preference for tan suits. The rebel of the group was twenty-nine-year-old Donais, a former investigator for a Parisian law firm. The lithe, five-foot-four blonde, who had shoulder-length hair, tended to wear trendy attire that flattered her shapely body. Today it was a short blue skirt and white knit sweater.

"How did you find us?" Bruno asked once they were seated.

"Your business address is listed on your investigator's license application, as well as your website, which, I might add, is spectacular."

Bruno smiled. He didn't bother to tell the deputy commissioner that the person who had designed and still maintained it was a former thief who had once resided in a prison not far from Acardi's own office.

"I'm sorry to barge in like this, but we need your help. Signora Nicchi's husband, Paolo, recently fell from a Conti Petroleum platform in the Adriatic Sea and drowned."

"I read about it. My sincere condolences," Donati said.

Bruno and Donais repeated Donati's sentiment. "A terrible accident," Donais said.

Dante Acardi shrugged in response to this remark, which piqued the three investigators' interest.

"How long did your husband work for Conti Petroleum?" Donati asked.

"Almost two years," the signora replied. "Prior to that, he'd been a geologist with BP for twenty-five years. However, when the oil spill in America occurred, the company made severe cuts in its staff, and he was forced into retirement. It didn't suit him. Paolo had no hobbies and very few friends, so he was very bored at home. When he heard that Conti Petroleum had an interest in drilling for gas in the Adriatic Sea and was looking for a marine geologist with experience in gas exploration, he applied. They hired him after one interview. He's been evaluating various undersea gas tracts for them ever since."

"How did you learn about his death, if you don't mind my asking?" Donais said.

"The police came to my home. They told me that there'd been an accident on the oil rig and that my Paolo had fallen into the water and died. At first, I didn't believe them."

"Why?" Donais inquired.

"I thought they had Paolo confused with someone else because he'd just returned the previous morning from his two-week shift and didn't have to report back to the rig for three weeks."

"When was the last time you saw your husband?" Bruno asked.

"I don't know exactly, but I think it was around ten thirty that night. He said that he was going to Taranto to see someone."

"That's late for a meeting," Bruno said.

"The person he was seeing was driving home from Naples and wouldn't get back until midnight. Paolo told me that the meeting was important and that he didn't want to wait until morning."

"Weren't you suspicious about your husband going somewhere at such a late hour?" Donais asked.

"Some women might believe their husband was seeing another woman," Lia Nicchi responded, picking up on Donais's implication. "But my husband wasn't having an affair. If he was, I would have sensed it."

Donais apologized for the question and thanked her for answering, after which Bruno asked Lia Nicchi to continue.

"Although I wasn't suspicious of what Paolo told me, I did ask him to stay the night in Taranto because he'd be very tired after the meeting, and the road between Taranto and Monopoli is not well lit and has many curves. That's why I wasn't concerned when he didn't come home." Lia Nicchi started sobbing.

Donais went into her room, retrieved a box of tissues, and offered the box to the widow.

"Grazie," Signora Nicchi responded, taking a tissue.

"Do you know who he was seeing in Taranto, or the reason for the meeting?" Donati asked.

"I didn't ask," she said apologetically.

"No need to apologize," Bruno replied sympathetically. "But if I'm understanding this correctly, your husband said that he had a meeting in Taranto but died in an accident on an oil rig off Monopoli. These cities, as I'm sure you know, are on opposite coasts." Bruno looked to Acardi and asked, "What's the distance between them?"

"Forty miles, more or less, as the crow flies."

"Did you ever discover why he went to the oil rig instead of Taranto?" Bruno asked.

"Not long after the police came, I received a call from Mr. Conti expressing his sympathies for Paolo's death. He said that he felt responsible because he'd called Paolo sometime after eleven that evening and asked him to return to the rig."

"Did he say why?" Donati asked.

"He said that he had an early morning conference call with investors who were interested in financing his gas exploration and production project. However, since the call had been scheduled at the last minute, he needed Paolo to come back to the rig and sit down with him to explain the technical data he'd compiled. He sent a helicopter to pick him up at the helipad in Monopoli." Nicchi paused to dab a tear that had worked its way down her right cheek.

"Did he say anything else?" Donais gently asked.

"Only that the company assumed full responsibility and would provide a monetary settlement that would ensure I'd be comfortable for the remainder of my life."

"I take it you're not buying this story," Bruno said, looking at Acardi.

"It sounds plausible. However, this tells me otherwise," Acardi said, pointing to his nose. "That's why we're here. One more thing," he said, removing an item from his briefcase.

Bruno looked at the three-by-three-inch piece of silver that was handed to him. After examining it, he handed the silver piece to Donati, who in turn passed it to Donais.

"What is it?" Donais asked, handing the object back to Bruno.

"I don't know. I've been referring to it as an artifact," Acardi said, "by definition, something of human construction that's not naturally present—in this case, something that shouldn't have been in Lia Nicchi's home but was."

"You found this in your house?" Bruno asked.

Lia Nicchi responded that she did.

"When?"

Acardi answered for her. "She found it on the floor of her husband's home office when she went to look for him, to see if he'd returned home while she was asleep. We believe it was dropped by someone between five and seven in the evening—that's when Lia and Paolo went to get groceries. It's the only time the house was unattended."

"What's this small emblem at the top?" Bruno asked, looking closely at the artifact.

"I don't have a clue. Hopefully, you'll be able to tell me."

"I take it, because you're here, that the Polizia di Stato isn't getting involved in this matter," Bruno stated.

"Based on the coroner's report, Paolo Nicchi's death was officially an accident. Therefore, with no proof of foul play and with our extensive workload and limited budget, I can't investigate his death. What I'd like your firm to do is determine what happened—pro bono of course, since Signora Nicchi is a widow and needs to save her money. Investigations can take time and, therefore, be expensive. Please help Lia because this"—Acardi pointed again to his nose—"is seldom wrong."

"Will you be working with us—unofficially, of course?" Bruno asked.

"I can't. I'm up to my neck in quicksand coordinating security for an upcoming NATO summit in Rome."

Bruno, Donati, and Donais exchanged glances that telegraphed their dismay: in addition to not getting paid, they couldn't count on getting information from Acardi that only the state police could provide.

Acardi seemed to sense their wariness. "I know this is going to cost your new firm not only money but also its most precious commodity—time. But there's no group of individuals in the world I trust more than the three of you. If you help me, I promise that the assistance and future referrals you'll receive will more than repay this kindness."

All three replied that they understood, bringing a smile of gratitude from Acardi.

"You realize that we're going to need to speak with Conti and also see where the accident took place," Bruno said, starting to list his ground rules.

"I'll make that happen, and if there's anyone else you want to see, I'll find the time to make those calls. Just find out the real story behind Paolo's death."

"Why are you so involved in this, Dante?" Bruno asked.

Acardi looked at Signora Nicchi standing beside him. "Because Lia is my sister."

Bruno, Donati, and Donais spent the rest of the day researching Antonio Conti and Paolo and Lia Nicchi online. In the process they developed a checklist of questions to be answered and tasks to be performed, then divided that list among themselves. Bruno and Donati would take a morning flight to the Bari Karol Wojtyła Airport, rent a car, and drive the forty miles to Monopoli, which didn't have an airport of its own. There they would go to the coroner's office and review the autopsy report, speak with Antonio Conti, and then look at the oil platform off which Paolo Nicchi had taken his fatal plunge. Bruno texted Acardi about this plan, and the deputy commissioner confirmed that he'd arrange for Conti and the coroner to make themselves available. During this time Donais would research the artifact that had been left with them.

As Bruno and Donati went to their rooms to pack, and Donais began searching the internet for objects that might be similar to the artifact in her hand, none knew that they would soon be knee-deep in a plot that would be the lead story for every media outlet in the world.

CHAPTER 3

GIANCARLO RAGNO, ITALY'S minister of justice, was five feet, one inch tall, weighed two hundred pounds, and shared the same vices as Paolo Nicchi—a lifetime of bad eating habits and lack of exercise. He was forty-five, and his hair was completely gray and rapidly disappearing. Married with four children, the Rome native had just finished with his mistress and was lying in bed as he watched the tall shapely brunette, who'd just turned nineteen, get dressed. He was under no illusion that she was with him because of love or the power of his position. Rather, it was because he paid for her lavish apartment and exorbitant shopping sprees, in addition to the cash stipend he provided each month. He was well compensated for his government position, but not enough to financially satisfy a mistress of the caliber of the one who'd lain beside him moments ago. Rather, it was the generous monthly payments to his offshore bank account from Antonio Conti that allowed him to partake of this and other vices.

He knew that taking money from the centimillionaire not only was illegal but also exposed him to possible discovery by one of the idealistic young lawyers who worked for him. They'd approached him on several occasions, concerned that they couldn't obtain the names of the investors behind the Swiss fund that had financed Conti Petroleum's growth. They expressed their fear that Conti could be laundering money and perhaps doing something much worse. If they only realized what an astute and correct assumption this was—especially the much worse aspect. Keeping the young attorneys at bay without creating suspicion of his involvement was arduous, but he only had to keep it up for two more years. After that he'd have enough money to pull the plug, escape his moribund family life, and move to a country without extradition where he could bribe government officials and the local police to do anything he wanted and afford a dozen mistresses who'd treat him like a king. No one was going to keep him from achieving that goal.

As he thought about his relationship with Conti, Ragno touched the piece of silver hanging from a chain around his neck. He and the oilman had met ten years ago at a government-industry function in Rome. At the time Ragno was a financially strapped attorney assigned to the immigration and naturalization section of the Ministry of Justice. He was surprised when Conti approached him. No one was ever interested in a low-level government employee, whose main reason for attending any government function was to partake of the free food and drink. The oilman struck up a conversation by asking his opinion on the current political climate, before segueing into how Ragno could fast-track citizenship for those who had skills critical to his company. Ragno recalled how, in a moment of inspiration that would change his life, he had said that he'd be happy to confidentially consult for Conti Petroleum and solve these issues for a monthly fee of $50,000. He had expected the oilman to either laugh and walk away or offer a substantially lower amount—which, considering his current financial situation, still would have been fine with Ragno. However, to his surprise, the oilman had agreed—which meant that Conti expected exponentially more services than those first suggested.

Over time, as Ragno ascended the ministry hierarchy to his current position, and his monthly consulting fee increased to $100,000, Conti had expanded his expectations. Ragno had to issue citizenship and passports to anyone Conti presented, find individuals specific jobs within the government, and ensure that there would be no investigation of Conti, his company, or anyone Conti referred to him. Ragno wasn't happy with these expectations, but he could live with them given the seven-figure yearly consulting fee he was receiving.

Looking at his watch, he noted the time and reluctantly pulled himself out of bed. As he did, the stunning brunette unbuttoned the top two buttons on her blouse, exposing her ample breasts. She then seductively walked across the room and gave him a long kiss. Knowing this was her way of asking for more money, he smiled as he took a wad of one-hundred-euro bills from his pocket, peeled off ten, and put the bills deep inside her jeans. God, how he loved being rich.

Bruno and Donati's EasyJet flight left Milan's Malpensa airport at 7:10 a.m. and arrived in Bari an hour and a half later. Since they had only carry-on baggage and were seated in the first row of economy, they were the first in line at Hertz, where Donati was assigned a Lancia Ypsilon. They got directions to Monopoli, which was twenty-nine miles away, and soon were entering the highway that paralleled the eastern coastline of the heel of Italy. To their left, as they drove south, was the Adriatic Sea, an intoxicatingly blue body of water that extended as far as they could see and separated the Italian and Balkan peninsulas. The sky was clear, the weather temperate, and the highway nearly deserted as they wove along the coast. Bruno and Donati began to decompress, loosening their ties and saying little to one another as they enjoyed the picturesque rocky shoreline. Thirty minutes later, they entered Monopoli, a city with a population of forty-nine thousand.

They checked into the Vecchio Mulino, a thirty-one-room hotel located in the heart of the city, and were given two adjoining rooms on the first floor. After dropping their bags off in their rooms, they went to the coroner's office, a ten-minute drive. The white rectangular building they entered had seen better days, having acquired a yellowish tint over the years from exposure to the sun and salt air of the nearby Adriatic Sea. The lobby, a ten-by-ten-foot area with worn and faded black linoleum flooring, was unmanned. Instead, a gray metal reception desk held a sign that directed anyone who wanted service to ring the bell beside the sign. Bruno did as directed, and less than a minute later, a man entered the lobby through a rear door and introduced himself as Ruggerio Amato, the city coroner.

Amato was in his midforties, was five feet, six inches in height, and had hazel eyes beneath thick bushy eyebrows. His hair, which came down to the bottom of his neck, was gray and fashionably cut. He might have been considered handsome except for the pronounced beer belly that protruded from his white lab coat and his pasty skin, which was as white as one of his cadaver's.

After Bruno and Donati introduced themselves, Amato said that he had received a phone call from Deputy Commissioner Acardi and had been told to provide them with anything they requested. He then led them back to his office, which was to the right of the reception desk.

The office was twenty-five feet to a side, and a small rectangular Formica-topped conference table sat to the left. The table looked as if it had been pilfered from a coffee shop, and the four chrome-legged and Naugahyde-covered chairs surrounding it completed that impression. To the right was a rectangular gray metal desk identical to the one in the lobby, dented in numerous places and devoid of papers and folders. Against the far wall were four file cabinets that matched the desks in color and condition.

Amato directed Bruno and Donati to the conference table, where he'd previously placed two copies of Paolo Nicchi's autopsy report in expectation of their visit. "Please take your time reading it," Amato said. "While you do, I'll get us an espresso."

After he left, Bruno and Donati delved into the report.

Apparently, getting anything to drink or eat required leaving the building, and Amato returned twenty minutes later carrying a tray with three cups of espresso, a small container of milk, and packets of sugar. Imprinted on the cups was the name of the café across the street. As Amato handed out the refreshments, none added anything to the rich liquid.

"It says that the decedent had chronic obstructive pulmonary disease, or COPD," Bruno said.

"He was definitely a heavy smoker. COPD, if you're not familiar with the disease, destroys a portion of the lung known as the alveoli, which is where the exchange of oxygen and carbon dioxide takes place. If you couple that with being overweight, walking for any distance, running, or climbing stairs would be a struggle. Mr. Nicchi wouldn't have been able to keep up that sort of activity for long before having to rest."

"I also see that his lungs had a trace amount of microplastics in them," Bruno said. "Isn't that unusual?"

"Somewhat. Microplastics are commonly found in the waters of the northern Ionian Sea. However, even though we're on the Adriatic side of the Apulia region, it's possible to have cross contamination since both seas converge south of us."

"If I understand the timeline," Donati said, "Nicchi is believed to have died at approximately 2:00 a.m., and the body was discovered at 3:00 a.m. and taken to the local hospital by a Conti Petroleum helicopter. Since the cause of death is listed here as drowning, are you saying that he survived a fall of"—Donati paused to look again at that section of the report—"one hundred and twenty feet?"

"He technically survived the fall but drowned within a few minutes," Amato said. "I say technically because his heart was still beating after he impacted the water, which is why the cause of death is drowning. However, since he broke both his legs and his arms in the fall and wasn't wearing a life jacket, he wouldn't have been able to raise his head above the choppy surface of the water. Drowning was inevitable."

"Is it unusual for someone working on an offshore platform to be on deck without a life jacket?" Bruno asked.

"From what I was told, it's against the rules. It's also against the rules for anyone on the platform to wear anything but antistatic clothing, given that a spark could prove cataclysmic for an oil platform."

"You're saying that he wasn't wearing antistatic clothing? How was he dressed when he was brought in?" Donati asked.

"The decedent was wearing a dress shirt, slacks, and shoes—extremely unusual attire for someone working in the pervasive oil and grime of an offshore platform."

"We were told that he was summoned back to the rig. He probably didn't have time to change or thought that he'd be taken home directly after his meeting," Donati said.

"That might explain it."

"The report indicates that you found alcohol in his system," Bruno said.

"A small amount, but not enough to affect muscular coordination or rational thought. I'd say he had the alcohol equivalent of one beer. There were also partially digested nuts in his stomach. He may have been eating those while drinking."

"Any suspicion of foul play?" Bruno asked.

"There's some bruising, especially on his knees, but nothing that's inconsistent with a fall of this nature. There was a large amount of lactic acid buildup in his body. However, since he fell twelve stories from an oil derrick and wasn't in shape to be climbing stairs, that wouldn't be out of the ordinary."

Bruno and Donati asked a few more questions and then left, an hour after they entered the building.

As Donati pulled the Lancia Ypsilon away from the curb and entered traffic, a black Fiat parked fifty yards behind them left the curb at the same time and entered the roadway.

"Is he still following us?" Bruno asked.

"The black Fiat 500X that tailed us from the airport?"

Bruno wasn't surprised by his partner's power of observation and smiled as Donati grinned in apparent satisfaction that he'd been aware of the Fiat from the start.

"Yes, he's still there," Donati said.

"Let's surprise him later and find out who he's working for."

"You've got my vote," Donati replied.

"I think it's time we visit the oil platform, speak with Antonio Conti, and see where Nicchi fell to his death," Bruno said.

Donati agreed. He pulled over to ask a local for the platform's location and then drove to the Conti Petroleum heliport. As they entered the ten-space parking lot, the black Fiat drove past and found an open spot on the street a little more than one hundred yards away. Since the vehicle's windows were tinted, neither Bruno nor Donati could see the face, or faces, of anyone inside.

They entered the heliport building, a single-story structure with a small sitting room and restroom and not much else. A man in his midtwenties, who had a beard that would have made Grizzly Adams proud, sat behind a cheap wooden desk a half dozen paces from the front door. Bruno and Donati gave their names and were told they were expected. This didn't come as a surprise to either; both had anticipated that Acardi would clear the way for them to see Conti.

While they sat down in the hemorrhoid-inducing wooden chairs in the waiting area, Grizzly Adams picked up a handheld phone off his desk and spoke into it. He apparently asked the pilot to come to the heliport because ten minutes later, they heard a helicopter set down behind the building. After handing Bruno and Donati each a life jacket, Grizzly Adams escorted them to the Airbus AS365 Dauphin. As they were strapping themselves into their seats, both stared at the large overhead hoist, to which a steel cable and web harness were attached, along with a control box. Moments later, the sliding door was slammed shut, and the helicopter rose off the helipad.

Lisette Donais looked at the three-by-three-inch piece of silver. Although she didn't wear jewelry—because in her profession she needed to avoid flash or anything that would call attention to herself over and above her natural beauty— she nevertheless liked it. Like most French women, she appreciated the classic and the elegant. However, the piece she was holding was neither. In fact, the five rows of unevenly spaced holes made it look like something one would find in a bazaar—unwanted and unloved until it was purchased by someone after reaching its lowest level of worth. Yet it was made of silver, which meant it was expensive and probably custom-made. She decided to take a closer look at the emblem that was etched at the top of it, which perhaps would give her a clue as to who had made it and lead her to the buyer.

Putting the artifact under a magnifying glass, Donais saw that the emblem was a globe with an open book above it. Emerging from the book were a rifle, a fist, and a flag. The workmanship was intricate, which solidified her belief that the piece was custom-made. Searching the internet, she was stunned to find that the emblem she was looking at was one of several symbols used by al-Qaeda in Iraq. Researching further, she found that the flag represented al-Qaeda's goal of creating an Islamic caliphate, and the rifle and fist represented its militancy. These symbols emerged from the Quran to indicate that the holy book was the foundation of their mission in Islam and to indicate al-Qaeda's intent to establish an Islamic state that included both Lebanon and Israel. The globe symbolized that their goals were worldwide.

After texting her discovery to Bruno and Donati, she looked again at the artifact and had a wild idea, based largely on a book she was reading. Looking through BD&D's consolidated contact list, she found the email address of the person who'd recently helped them solve a case and get the murder charges against her partners dropped. Taking a photo of the artifact with her cell phone, she sent this to him along with her thoughts as to what the artifact might be. If this person could confirm her suspicions, then this might be the break they needed to find out what had really happened to Paolo Nicchi. If she was wrong, and her contact thought that what she'd sent him was a photo of an ugly piece of jewelry and nothing more, then she was no worse off.

Once the email was sent, she decided that nothing more could be accomplished in Milan. Not willing to stay in the office while her partners got to do fieldwork, she packed a carry-on bag and hailed a taxi. An hour later, she was at the airport and through security. She couldn't wait to see the look on her partners' faces when she surprised them.

CHAPTER 4

THE TUMI LATITUDE suitcase had been delivered to Sargon Zebari by a brigadier general in the Iranian army. The lightweight bag made from woven ballistic material could be purchased at any luggage shop. What was inside could not. The container of iridium—a radioactive material used in the radiological industry—the block of C-4 explosive, a remotely controlled detonator, and a cell phone with a preset phone number that would initiate detonation had been assembled in Tehran, designed to be an especially dirty weapon of mass disruption that would render a wide area unfit for human habitation.

Zebari and his radioactive cargo were put on an Iranian military aircraft and flown from Tehran to Damascus. From there he was transported to a small landing strip on the Gulf of Sidra, off the coast of Libya, where a submarine took him to an anchored Panamanian-flagged merchant vessel, the *Capira*, which Conti routinely used to smuggle men and weapons into Italy. The Panamanian-flagged merchant ship, which was indirectly owned by the Iranian government, was a 431-foot-long and 54-foot-wide powered piece of rust that had been built in the 1990s and had received little maintenance since. En route to the port of Durres, Albania, the ship briefly stopped in the narrow seaway between the Ionian and Adriatic Seas, where Rotolo, piloting a small oceangoing oil barge, met Zebari and took possession of the suitcase. Rotolo then returned to the oil platform, where Conti kept his office, arriving thirty minutes ahead of Bruno and Donati.

The helicopter carrying the Italian investigators set down on the helipad of the tension-leg oil platform, which was permanently tethered to the seabed one thousand feet below. This type of anchoring eliminated virtually all vertical movement, allowing the platform to use risers and have production wellheads on deck. Once the rotors came to a stop, someone slid open the helicopter door from outside and introduced himself as Armanno Rotolo, the company's chief operating officer. Bruno had dealt with bureaucrats and corporate types his entire life, but the expressionless face, the darting eyes, and the bulge in the back of Rotolo's jacket, which indicated he was carrying a weapon, led him to believe that the person greeting them had additional responsibilities that were probably not suitable for a corporate résumé.

After everyone shook hands, Rotolo told them that he was taking them to Antonio Conti's office-apartment. Walking to a steel stairway, they ascended one deck to a watertight entry door. Inside was a hallway with doors on both sides, each stenciled with a number. Rotolo knocked on the first door, marked "01," and entered without waiting for a response.

Bruno's eyes widened, and his mouth fell slightly open. His first impression was one of surprise because he had assumed that any space occupied by someone as wealthy as Conti would be opulent, even on an oil platform. The fact that it was spartan and basic caused him to suddenly stop and take a closer look at the room he was entering. The office was twenty by fifteen feet. In front of him was a dark wooden desk that was scratched, chipped, and worn from years of use and abuse. Next to it was a rectangular table with four chairs, in the same condition as the desk. To the right he saw an open doorway that led to what looked to be a bedroom and bathroom, which appeared to be half the size of the office. The walls were painted gray, and affixed to them, from two feet to six feet off the floor, were large rectangular corkboards containing technical data and drawings. The floors were coated with black nonslip rubber, which was easier to clean and maintain than conventional flooring, given that they were on an oil rig.

Conti, who was wearing black antistatic multipocket work trousers and a black long-sleeved antistatic work shirt and matching jacket, the same as Rotolo, came from around his desk to greet them. After introductions were exchanged, the four men sat at the table.

"You can take off those life jackets, if you like," Rotolo said. "It's only a requirement that they be worn on the outside platform and in the helicopter."

Bruno and Donati complied and placed the jackets in Rotolo's outstretched hand.

"I received a call from Deputy Commissioner Acardi indicating that you're investigating the accidental death of Paolo Nicchi. I looked at your website and did a Google search on you both as well. You've had very impressive careers with the state police. That said, I'm afraid your talents are wasted here. Paolo's death, while tragic, was an accident. The local police in Monopoli have concluded as much, and I'm sure they can give you a copy of their findings."

Bruno said that he understood, but since the accident had occurred offshore, the state police had decided that a more detailed investigation was mandated. He said that their firm had been given this assignment because the matter was considered a noncritical investigation and didn't warrant burdening state police investigators, who already had a backlog of cases awaiting their attention. That was garbage, but from the looks on Conti and Rotolo's faces, this response satisfied them.

Bruno started his questioning by asking how many people worked on the rig.

"We have a crew of forty aboard this platform, half of whom are on duty at any given time," Rotolo answered. "They work two weeks on and two weeks off unless they occupy a skilled position, in which case they're given three weeks off. Paolo Nicchi was one such employee. This rig is unusual in that everyone who works on it, except for Paolo, is single and chooses to live on board full-time. Therefore, they seldom go to Monopoli. I'm told the reason for this is that food and lodging are free here, making an apartment in Monopoli redundant and an unnecessary expense. Also, unlike most platforms, which have dormitories that sleep four to eight crew members, all our employees have their own room."

"Aren't men in this profession generally young?" Donati asked. "Doesn't living on board take away their social life— such as going out with women, drinking, and so on?"

"They're young, but they're here for a purpose—to make money as quickly as possible so they can leave with a great deal of cash. However, I should note that their work here comes with several sacrifices," Rotolo said. "For example, guests are not permitted on the platform unless approved by management. That said, the company tends to give crew members substantial leeway as to whom they can bring on board. However, alcohol and nonprescription drugs are prohibited, and if anyone is caught with either, they're immediately terminated. Smoking is allowed for those who must get their nicotine fix, but only in the designated area, where we provide matches. Cigarette lighters and anything else that initiates a flame or gets hot enough to start a fire are prohibited from being brought onto the rig."

"How much are the men paid?" Donati asked.

"The average annual wage per employee is $93,000, with the standard workday being a twelve-hour shift," said Rotolo. "Since Paolo Nicchi was in a skilled position, he earned $120,000 per year."

Bruno looked to Conti and asked, "Do you extract both oil and gas from this platform?"

"For the moment, only oil. We intend to begin extracting gas in the future, which is what Paolo had been focused on for the past two years."

"According to Lia Nicchi, you told her that you phoned her husband late at night and asked that he return to the rig. What was that about?" Bruno asked, not revealing what he already knew.

"Funding oil and gas projects, particularly when they're offshore, is extremely expensive, and this company doesn't currently have the funds for such an endeavor," Conti explained. "Therefore, we rely on outside investors who, unlike a bank, will take the risk for the possibility of an extraordinary return. I don't know if you've ever dealt with investors before, Mr. Bruno, but you have only one shot to make your pitch and convince them. Therefore, I needed to make sure I understood the data Paolo had been compiling. This needed to be done in person since charts are extremely difficult to discuss on the phone."

"I'm curious—did the call go well?" Donati asked.

"We have our investor thanks to Paolo's work."

"Did you know that Paolo was going to Taranto before you phoned him?"

"I didn't. Why was he going to Taranto?"

"I was hoping that you could tell us," Donati said.

"I'm sorry, but I can't. When I phoned Paolo, he said that he'd drive to the helipad and that he'd be there in less than thirty minutes. I assumed he was in bed when I called and needed to get dressed."

"How long did your meeting last?" Bruno asked.

"I can't remember exactly," Conti answered. "I would say about an hour and a half, more or less."

"That would make it 1:30 a.m.—more or less," Bruno replied. "The coroner placed the time of death at around 2:00 a.m. If your meeting was finished thirty minutes prior to that, why didn't he go back ashore and then home?"

"I loved Paolo, but he had two bad habits: eating and smoking. I didn't see where he went after the meeting, but I assume it was to the kitchen for an early morning snack, or atop the derrick to have a smoke while looking at the lights in Monopoli—it's a lovely view."

"Do people normally smoke atop the derrick?" Bruno asked.

"No. In fact, as Rotolo said, there's only one designated smoking area on this rig, and it's not far from the helipad. However, over the years the derrick has become a second unofficial venue for smokers. Again, the view of the Adriatic Sea and Monopoli is nice for anyone who's willing to endure the climb."

"The helicopter pilot wasn't suspicious about the length of time he had to wait?" Donati asked.

"He didn't know how long the meeting would last. After securing the helicopter on the helipad, he went to the kitchen to get a bite to eat and then to the common area to watch a movie while he waited for Paolo to summon him for the return flight. He was on duty, so it was irrelevant whether he was here or at the heliport in Monopoli."

Although Conti's responses were reasonable, they seemed practiced and robotic. Bruno changed the subject to try to catch Conti off guard.

"I wonder if you can identify this for me?" Bruno asked. Taking his cell phone from his pocket, he accessed the photo he'd taken of the piece of silver and showed it to Conti. "This was found in Paolo Nicchi's house. Have you ever seen this before?"

Bruno looked closely at Conti, who had yet to take a breath since looking at the photo.

"No. What is it?"

"I'm not entirely sure, but the emblem, according to our partner, is used by al-Qaeda in Iraq."

"That's curious," Conti said, not exhibiting any surprise at being told that something possibly linked to al-Qaeda had been discovered in the home of one of his employees.

"Do you have this object with you so I can examine it more closely?" Conti asked.

"I didn't bring it, but it's in a safe place."

When Conti went silent, indicating he didn't want to speak about the mysterious piece of silver any further, Bruno suggested that this would be a good time to see where the accident had occurred.

Rotolo went to a two-drawer cabinet behind Conti's desk and removed two pairs of antistatic pants and corresponding jackets, which matched the attire, minus the shirts, that he and Conti were wearing. He handed Bruno and Donati each a set. "You can slip these on over your clothes and then put on your life jacket," Rotolo said. "We don't permit anyone on deck without antistatic gear and an inflatable life jacket."

Bruno and Donati weren't in bad shape, but the twelve-story climb up the steep stairway left them gasping for breath and their legs aching by the time they reached the upper deck, which was 125 feet above the water. They could see Monopoli in the distance, a view that was undoubtedly more impressive at night.

"My leg muscles are killing me," Bruno said, "and being an ex-smoker, I can tell you that I'm also light-headed. That makes me question why a significantly overweight man would come up here, view or no view. On top of that, he wasn't wearing an antistatic suit or a life jacket."

"When Paolo met with me in my office," Conti answered, "I didn't require him to don the antistatic gear because he was only going to and from the helicopter. I didn't think he'd go anywhere else on the rig. As for the life jacket, he took his off when he entered my office, the same as you. We carry spare vests on the helicopter. The pilot would have handed him one before they took off."

"Did anyone see him climb the derrick?" Bruno asked.

"I questioned each man who was on duty that night," Rotolo responded. "No one saw him. As a matter of practicality, since we're not drilling anymore because we're in production, workers seldom look at the derrick from which Paolo fell. They're busy trying to keep everything running on deck."

"Then no one saw him fall?" Donati asked.

"As I said," Rotolo replied, in a tone that indicated he was growing weary of being questioned, "no one noticed him on the derrick."

"Then how do you know he fell from here?" Donati asked.

"With his arms and legs broken, he looked like a rag doll when we fished him out of the water. Knowing he was a smoker, and looking at the damage to his body, I put two and two together. I also told this to the coroner."

"Who found the body?" Donati continued.

"I did," Rotolo answered.

"How did you see him in the water at that hour since he wasn't wearing reflective gear? Come to think of it, how did he fall into the water? This derrick is ten feet from the edge of the platform. Nicchi was a rock—he couldn't have tripped more than ten inches."

"To answer your first question, there are lights that illuminate a ten-foot radius around the platform. I saw Nicchi's body within this perimeter. In answer to your second question, I can't explain how he fell from the derrick and into the water. I suspect that he hit the deck and rolled off the platform. As you can see, there's only a double chain along the edge. If Nicchi had a muscle cramp, for example," Rotolo said, looking Bruno straight in the eye without flinching a muscle, "then he might have tripped or stumbled off this deck, and his momentum would have carried him into the Adriatic."

"If I fell from this height, I wouldn't roll—I'd splatter," Bruno said, not believing a word of what he was being told. "Can we see Nicchi's room?" he asked.

Conti, probably grateful to get away from this line of questioning, led the way, with Rotolo bringing up the rear.

They entered Nicchi's quarters, a fifteen-by-fifteen-foot room with a bed wide enough for one person, a small desk and chair, and a wall-mounted TV. The floor was covered with the same rubberized material as Conti's office-apartment, and the furniture appeared to have the same provenance. Donati did a quick inspection of the desk. He pulled out each of the drawers but found nothing inside or underneath.

"All Paolo's personal items were sent to his wife," Rotolo said, seeming to sense Donati's impending question about why the room was empty.

"Who packed his belongings?" Donati asked.

"I did," Rotolo replied.

"What were his personal effects?"

"Clothing, shaving gear, a comb, a pocketknife, several books—not much more."

"What about a cell phone? He must have had one, because you called and told him to return to the rig."

"I didn't find one in his room," Rotolo said. "It may have gone into the water when he fell."

"Is the kitchen open all night?" Donati asked.

"This rig operates 24/7, so the kitchen never closes," Rotolo answered.

"Then if someone is hungry between meals, they can go there for a snack."

"That's correct."

"That said, did Nicchi have any snacks in his room?"

"None."

"No beer nuts, peanuts, or anything of this nature?"

"We don't permit our kitchen to carry processed foods," Conti interjected. "They tend to make the men fat and lethargic. Instead, we have only whole foods—vegetables, fruits, meat, fish, poultry, and eggs that have not been processed."

"It certainly seems as if Paolo fell off the wagon when he went home," Bruno said.

Conti ignored the remark. They left Nicchi's room, and Rotolo continued the tour of the platform, taking Bruno and Donati to the rig's operations center, kitchen, and common areas before everyone returned to Conti's office. There Bruno and Donati took off their antistatic gear, donned their life jackets, and returned to the helicopter.

After seeing Bruno and Donati to the helipad, Conti returned to his office, followed by Rotolo.

"What do you think?" Rotolo asked.

"They've been detectives long enough to spot a cover-up. They don't believe Nicchi's death was an accident. And since they know about Taranto, they'll probably go there. When they do, I have no doubt that they'll find his car. From what I hear, the vehicle won't be hard to find because it has yellow police tape wrapped around it. After that, they'll know I lied to them."

"There was no way for us to get the vehicle because as soon as the police arrived, they cordoned off the only two cars in the tavern's parking lot—one belonging to the reporter and the other to Nicchi."

"What worries me is that Bruno and Donati will pass what they find and suspect to Acardi. After that, no matter how much the minister of justice might try to intervene to squelch an investigation, the state police will ignore him and probe us so deeply that we won't be able to carry out our plan."

"When do you think they'll call Acardi?" Rotolo asked.

"For all I know, they already have. But I believe they'll want to give him something concrete, which means they'll wait until they find Nicchi's car. Until then, they're only guessing."

"So, we kill them."

"Not only them, but their other partner who has the template. No loose ends. I don't care if it looks like an accident or not—just make sure it's done quickly."

CHAPTER 5

CAPTAIN GREGORIO XENOS was a third-generation seafarer from the small town of Limni, in the northwestern portion of the Greek island of Euboea. He was five feet, seven inches tall and weighed 180 pounds, and his hair and beard were completely gray. Fifty-five years old, Xenos had never married, having been employed on commercial ships since he was fifteen, except for his time spent attending a merchant marine academy. For the past three years he'd been the captain of the *Trochus*, a 1,132-long, 177-foot-wide, 114-foot-high liquefied natural gas carrier that had a draft of thirty-nine feet. After the gas was converted to a liquid, which took up 1/600th of the volume of natural gas in a gaseous state, and its temperature was brought down to minus 260 degrees Fahrenheit, the liquefied natural gas, or LNG, was transferred to six spherical tanks located along the centerline of the ship. Each tank was surrounded by ballast tanks, cofferdams, and voids that gave the *Trochus*, for all practical purposes, a second hull.

Sixteen days ago, Xenos had taken on 5.5 million cubic feet of LNG in Doha, Qatar, and was now twenty-two hours away from the Italian port of Civitavecchia, which was approximately fifty miles from the center of Rome. Every system on the ship was operating perfectly, and the seas were forecasted to be calm along the *Trochus*'s route. That was good news for the residents of Rome and its surrounding population centers. The last LNG carrier en route to Civitavecchia had experienced a series of catastrophic equipment failures—thanks, unbeknownst to Captain Xenos, to a large bribe paid by Antonio Conti to the ship's chief engineer. The result was that it had had to be towed back to Doha. That was three months ago. Because demand for LNG carriers was high and schedules were tight, Rome had been unable to get a replacement shipment prior to the *Trochus*, and the natural gas supply in Civitavecchia was running perilously low.

Now, although Captain Gregorio Xenos didn't know it, the *Trochus* was Conti's lead domino for setting off a chain of events that would make the 9/11 attacks seem minuscule by comparison.

"Did you get the impression that Conti's hiding something?" Donati asked as he looked in his rearview mirror and saw that the Fiat 500X was again following them.

"I noticed that whenever we spoke about Nicchi, he didn't make eye contact with us. He also fidgeted like someone who was late for a meeting, cleared his throat throughout our conversation, and changed the pitch of his voice every other sentence. He's a textbook example of what to look for when someone is lying."

"Factually," Donati added, "there are several things that still need to be explained about Nicchi's death. For example, why was he on the derrick, if he ever was? How did he end up in the Adriatic? I don't believe he'd roll ten feet off the platform after hitting the deck. What about the presence of microplastics in his lungs? How did he consume beer nuts and an alcoholic beverage on a platform that didn't contain either?"

"The autopsy report indicated a fall from approximately 125 feet into the water," Bruno said. "If he didn't fall from the derrick, and it seems likely he didn't, then what else was at that height and adjacent to the water?"

After a moment, Bruno and Donati exclaimed almost simultaneously, "The helicopter!"

"Let's assume that he was thrown out of a helicopter," Bruno said. "Let's further assume it happened on the Ionian Sea, the western side of the Apulia, since the autopsy report indicated the presence of microplastics in his lungs. He was taken to the hospital in Monopoli by a Conti Petroleum helicopter. Maybe he was first thrown out of it to create the illusion that he fell from the derrick. Murders get investigated in painstaking detail; accidents don't."

"Perhaps he never returned to Monopoli but was killed in Taranto," said Donati. "What's open at midnight that serves beer and nuts?"

"Sounds like a bar," Bruno answered. "And if Nicchi is dead, what about the person he was going to meet? Was that person also killed?"

"I'd say he's also plucking a harp," Donati answered.

"I have an idea about how we can find out."

Bruno took his cell phone from his pocket and called Ruggerio Amato. He asked the coroner if he had a listing of deaths in Taranto that had occurred the night before, or on the day that Nicchi died. Meanwhile, Donati pulled into the parking lot of their hotel and shut off the engine.

After Bruno ended his call, he said, "I think we might have something. Amato accessed his coroner database and found that a reporter, Domenico Marchetti, was shot and killed in Taranto just hours before Nicchi died."

"Looks like we know who Nicchi saw."

"Let's say Conti learned of the meeting and knew or suspected the subject of their conversation, which had to be something extremely serious for him to order the deaths of both men."

"Something that would land him in jail or destroy his company," Donati continued. "He dispatches a killer in his helicopter to silence both men, probably Rotolo since he looks more like an assassin than a COO."

Bruno nodded. "He kills the reporter and orchestrates Nicchi's death as a drowning on the other coast so no one will connect the dots between Nicchi and Marchetti. The last thing Conti wants is both men killed in the same place at the same time. A double homicide attracts a lot of attention and would launch a state police investigation, not to mention that the newspaper the reporter worked for would launch its own investigation as well."

"I don't know if the facts fit the story or we created a story to fit the facts," said Donati. "Either way, I think we should run with it."

"Let's begin by going to the spot where the reporter was killed and see if anyone in that area recognizes Nicchi or Marchetti. I'll get Lisette to find photos of them and text them to us," Bruno said.

As Bruno accessed Google Maps to get directions to Taranto, Donati started the engine and pulled out of the hotel parking lot. Entering the main highway, he looked in his rearview mirror and saw that the Fiat 500X had settled in fifty yards behind them. Forty minutes later, everyone entered Taranto.

Rotolo looked at his computer screen and, thanks to the tracker the heliport attendant had installed under the investigators' car, saw where Bruno and Donati were headed. Summoning two of the men working on the rig to his quarters, he ordered them to kill the intrusive investigators, even if it meant sacrificing their own lives. Both men were former Iraqi fighters and devout members of al-Qaeda, so neither had a problem with that order. He gave both men suppressed handguns, provided a photo of Bruno and Donati that he had taken from the rig's security camera, and taught them how to track their prey through an app on the burner phone he provided. He also told them that once they'd completed this assignment, they must go to Milan to kill private investigator Lisette Donais. Before they did, however, they were to get from her, by whatever means necessary, the location of a three-by-three-inch piece of silver with holes in it. She wasn't to die before then. Both men were expressionless as they received these instructions.

"The weapons you'll need, along with Donais's address, are on the helicopter," Rotolo said. "Once you kill Bruno and Donati, the pilot will fly you to Milan."

Rotolo escorted the men onto the helicopter, which was sitting on the helipad with its rotors turning, and watched them board. Immediately, the Dauphin lifted off and accelerated toward Taranto.

As Donais stepped off her flight at the Bari Karol Wojtyła Airport, she turned on her cell phone and found that Bruno had asked her to send photos of both Nicchi and Marchetti, a reporter who had been killed in Taranto the same day that Nicchi died. Donais quickly found their photos in the obituary sections of their local newspapers and texted these pictures to both Bruno and Donati.

Deciding to delay checking into the hotel in Monopoli, Donais went to the rental car center at the airport. The twenty-year-old employee at the counter was apparently taken with the attractive woman in front of him because when she requested the cheapest car available, he gave her a red Fiat 124 Spider roadster, which rented for three times the rate of the chunkier cars in her price category, and ignored the price difference.

Once she had loaded her overnight bag into the vehicle's minuscule trunk, Donais looked at the "Find Friends" locator app on her phone and saw that Bruno and Donati were on a road leading to Taranto. Putting that destination into her GPS system, which indicated that she was 39.1 miles away, she put the pedal to the metal and roared out of the rental car lot.

Bruno and Donati parked their car in a small parking lot beside the Tre Taverne, named after a reception center for travelers on the ancient Appian Way. Since it was just yards from the site of Marchetti's murder and the only bar within view, they decided to start their search here.

When the bartender came to take their order, Bruno told him that he and his colleague had been sent by the state police to investigate the murder of Domenico Marchetti and asked to speak with whoever was on duty the night of the murder. Although that was stretching the truth to the point where the rubber band almost broke, Bruno sounded convincing, and the man never asked to see a badge. As fate would have it, the person they were speaking with had worked the night the reporter was murdered. Bruno asked if they could ask him a couple of questions, and the bartender agreed and summoned one of the two waitresses on duty to take his place. He then motioned Bruno and Donati to a nearby table.

"Do you recognize these two men?" Donati asked, pulling his phone from his jacket pocket and showing the bartender the obituary photos of Nicchi and Marchetti that Donais had sent.

"They were both here the night this one"—the bartender put his finger on the image of Marchetti—"was killed. They sat at that corner booth." He pointed to a table at the far end of the tavern. "As I recall, each had a Peroni and went through a couple of bowls of these nuts," he said, looking down to the similar bowl on their table. "They seemed to be here to talk, not to drink."

"Anything else you remember?" Bruno asked.

"They were the last two to leave the bar. Shortly after they left, I put the cash in the safe and locked up. That was a little after 2:00 a.m. The waitresses left two hours earlier, when we stopped serving food."

"The autopsy report said that you discovered the body," Bruno said.

"I locked the front door and was on my way to my car when I saw a man lying on the ground. I ran to him, but I knew he was dead when I saw a bullet hole in the center of his forehead. I called the police, and after I gave them a statement, I left."

"You said they were talking rather than drinking," Bruno said. "Did they exchange anything?"

"The heavier-set of the two men, as I recall, came in with a folder. I remember because this tavern doesn't cater to business types. Businessmen go to the more gentrified establishments a mile or so away. This is a workingman's bar.

The only thing people sometimes carry in here is a chip on their shoulder. I do remember that when they left, the man who was killed was carrying the folder."

"And the two men seemed friendly and didn't argue?"

"No arguments, at least from what I saw."

"You have a good memory," Donati said.

"When someone is killed, it tends to jog one's memory."

"Good point," Donati conceded.

After the bartender said that was all he could remember, they thanked him and left the tavern.

"Conti has some explaining to do," Bruno said. "If Nicchi was here at two in the morning, he couldn't have been on the rig, as Conti told us. I'm guessing that if we get hold of Nicchi's phone records, we won't find that call from Conti."

"I'm not going to take that bet, but I will call Acardi and have him get Nicchi's phone records for us," Donati replied.

"That means," Bruno said, "that he was probably thrown out of the helicopter somewhere off the Taranto coast, and his body was recovered and returned to Monopoli so that it would appear he died in a work accident. That way no one would be able to connect the two deaths."

Bruno and Donati walked about ten feet from the tavern's entrance, to where the autopsy report indicated Marchetti had been murdered. The pair looked around. The site of the murder had apparently been cleaned because no blood was visible.

"Let's think about this," Bruno said. "The reporter was killed here, not long after he left the tavern. Presumably, since the autopsy didn't mention a folder being recovered, the killer took the folder. The coroner also said that Nicchi had a high level of lactic acid in his system. Conti would have us believe that it was from climbing the stairs to the top of the derrick.

However, it's more likely that the lactic acid buildup was from trying to run away from the killer."

"Who eventually caught up with him," said Donati, "which probably wasn't all that difficult given what we know about Nicchi's physical limitations."

Both men were still considering their latest interpretation of what had happened when the bartender walked outside carrying a large manila envelope.

"I was hoping you'd still be here," he said. "One of the waitresses told me that the morning cleanup crew found what's inside this envelope in the booth where the two people you were asking about sat." Handing the envelope to Bruno, he continued, "She put it in the supply room for safekeeping and forgot about it till just now, when she asked me who you both were."

Bruno saw that "Table 12" had been written on the outside of the envelope, with the date of the dead men's visit to the bar written below. Bruno thanked the bartender, and once the man had gone back inside, he opened the envelope. Inside was an eight-by-ten photo of Antonio Conti standing beside an arms crate that was being loaded onto his helicopter.

"I think we now know why Conti wanted both men killed," Bruno said. "It appears he's using his oil platform to smuggle arms, and possibly much more, into the country."

As Bruno was putting the photo back into the envelope, two formidable-looking men approached. Each had a silenced handgun, and they motioned with their weapons for Bruno and Donati to go to the parking lot. The fact that both men not only held their weapons with comfortable assurance but also kept just far enough away to prevent either Bruno or Donati from turning and grabbing the weapons indicated that killing wasn't foreign to them.

They'd gone ten yards into the lot when one of the men ordered them to stop. He grabbed the envelope from Bruno's right hand, opened it, and looked at the photo. While his partner kept his gun trained on them, the man took a lighter from his pocket and set fire to the photograph. Once it had been reduced to cinders, he scuffed the burnt remains with the bottom of his shoe until what remained was little more than a dark gray smudge.

The two men, neither of whom was a talker apparently, adjusted their weapons so that the rounds would impact the chests of their targets. Bruno and Donati's bodies noticeably tensed, although they maintained eye contact with the killers. When the two gunshots in rapid succession occurred, both men looked down at their chests, surprised to be unharmed. Even more surprising was that both would-be executioners were lying dead on the ground in front of them. Looking beyond them, thirty yards in the distance, they saw a man holding a scoped rifle beside a black Fiat 500X. Next to him was the familiar figure of Lisette Donais, who was also holding a scoped rifle.

Their savior was twenty-five years old and five feet, eleven inches tall, with short black hair and brown eyes. He weighed 180 pounds and had broad shoulders, a narrow waist, and in most women's eyes, just enough stubble on his face to be considered ruggedly handsome. He introduced himself as Gabriel Messina, a state police chief superintendent.

Messina walked to the bodies and kicked both men's weapons away, then checked each body for a pulse. The eyes of both scumbags were open in a permanent stare of surprise and disbelief, and the entrance wounds in their backs were a fifth the size of the exit wounds, so Messina shouldered his weapon. He then searched their bodies, finding only a lighter and pack of cigarettes on one and a three-inch folding knife on the other.

"Nice timing. Do you always carry more than one rifle in your vehicle?" Bruno asked, noting that he and Donais had the same weapon.

"I sometimes have a partner. I carry a small arsenal in the trunk of my car because I constantly run into smugglers, human traffickers, and other nefarious characters along the Taranto coast. I never want to be outgunned."

"Do I have Dante Acardi to thank for you following us?" Bruno inquired.

"He told me that you both were the best officers who ever worked for him but said you attract trouble like a magnet. He also said that I should take some vacation time and use it to follow and protect you, but not tell anyone at my station what I was doing."

"Have you known the deputy commissioner long?"

"My whole life. Dante Acardi is my uncle. Let me call this in," Messina said, breaking off the conversation as he walked back to his vehicle.

Messina went to his Fiat, which turned out to be an unmarked police cruiser, and called the dispatcher. A few minutes later, several police cars showed up, lights blazing. It took two hours for the bodies and area surrounding them to be photographed, for the on-site paperwork to be completed, for the coroner to certify that the men were dead, and for a black station wagon to take the bodies away.

Messina was leaning against his Fiat 500X when Bruno, Donati, and Donais approached. "I spoke with my uncle and told him what happened. He asked me to keep this incident between the four of us. Therefore, my report will say that as I was driving by this tavern, I came upon two men trying to rob the both of you at gunpoint. I ordered them to drop their weapons, and when they refused and pointed their guns in my direction, I fired."

"They were killed with two different rifles," Bruno pointed out. "Also, the bullets entered their backs and not their chests."

"Two men with silenced weapons were shot and killed by a local officer of the law while they were trying to rob two retired police officers. No one is going to conduct a ballistics test or care how they died. Case closed."

Bruno and Donati both nodded in agreement. Case closed.

"What's that?" Donati asked Messina, gesturing toward two cars in the lot with yellow police tape around them.

"One vehicle, I forget which one, belongs to the reporter who was killed here the other night, and the other was the only other vehicle in the tavern's parking lot when my colleagues arrived at the murder scene. They should be picked up soon and brought to the impound yard."

They all walked to the vehicles.

"Want to bet one of these belongs to Paolo Nicchi?" Bruno said.

"Which puts another hole in Conti's claim that he was on the rig," said Donati.

"Let's go back to the hotel and piece what we have together," Bruno said.

"Agreed."

Bruno then turned toward Messina. "We're going back to our hotel in Monopoli to talk about all this. Care to join us?"

"I have to file a report at the station, but I'll join you as quickly as possible after that," Messina said, and he turned to walk back to his vehicle.

"How does the Spider drive?" Donati asked Donais.

"Fantastic."

Donati handed Bruno the key to their Lancia Ypsilon and followed Donais to her vehicle. Moments later, with Donati at the wheel, the roadster roared past Bruno.

CHAPTER 6

THE QUIRINAL PALACE, which most Italians referred to as simply the Quirinal, was the residence of the president of the Italian Republic. Built in 1853 by Pope Gregory XII as a papal summer residence and located on Quirinal Hill, the 1.1-million-square-foot structure was the largest residence in the world for a head of state. Security within, around, and below it was always tight. Recently, that had increased exponentially as the Italian army, state police, and advance security teams from twenty-nine countries implemented advanced security protocols in preparation for an upcoming NATO summit that would be held there. Tomorrow the presidents of the United States and Italy, the prime minister of Great Britain, the chancellor of Germany, and a host of other representatives from all twenty-nine NATO member nations would come together to discuss new policies and initiatives to modernize the seventy-year-old organization.

In preparation for the summit, the vast areas below and within the historic residence, as well as the hotels in which the heads of state would be staying, were fitted with sensors that could detect explosive devices, lethal biological and chemical agents, and any other agent that could potentially harm those at the summit. In addition, manhole covers within two blocks of these areas were welded shut. Last, the Italians installed a barrier against human intrusion, consisting of General Electric M134 miniguns that hung from the ceilings in the subterranean cavities beneath these locations. Each minigun was a six-barrel electrically driven and belt-fed Gatling gun that fired 6,000 rounds per minute at a velocity of 2,850 feet per second up to a distance of 3,280 feet. Each was controlled by an operator at an undisclosed off-site command post. Patrolling the skies above these areas were three Italian Army Agusta A129 Mangusta attack helicopters, each equipped with 81 mm unguided rockets, fourth-generation antitank missiles, and a three-barrel M197 electric cannon.

Rotolo informed Conti of the failed attempt to kill Bruno and Donati and the deaths of their two Muslim brothers. Conti, in an uncharacteristic show of emotion, slammed his fist down hard on his desk.

"Let me kill them," Rotolo said as Conti regained his composure.

"As tempting as that is," said Conti, "with less than forty-eight hours to go before we initiate our plan against NATO and its allies, we need to keep our distance and stay in the background. The fact that the state police are indirectly delving into Nicchi's death by using those investigators means that they're looking at us."

"Bruno and Donati probably know by now that we've been lying to them about Paolo being on the platform the night he died. That makes them dangerous and a threat to our plan."

"They're exceptionally dangerous," Conti corrected. "However, killing them so soon after a previous attempt on their lives might focus attention on Nicchi and therefore on me. It seems that another approach is in order. We don't necessarily need their deaths to keep them out of our way for two days, although death is always the preferential way of keeping a secret. In two days, you'll have my permission to kill Bruno, Donati, and this Donais person as well."

"How do we keep them from looking into us and interfering with our operation until then?"

Conti told him.

Giancarlo Ragno had earlier decrypted an email from Conti asking him to courier a suitcase to Washington, DC, a transport made considerably more complicated by the billionaire's instructions that the suitcase must bypass American customs and couldn't be x-rayed. As a reward for this favor, Conti's email explained, one million dollars had been wired into Ragno's offshore bank account, a fact the rotund government official verified. Given the amount of money he'd been given, Ragno wasn't about to disappoint his benefactor.

It took an hour for him to come up with a plan. The minister of justice concluded that one entity could guarantee that what he was transporting would remain secret when it crossed another country's border. He had a good working relationship with the minister of foreign affairs and felt certain that he could get a temporary diplomatic passport issued to him and what he was carrying designated as a diplomatic pouch. However, no political favor was free of charge. Fortunately, Ragno had a huge bargaining chip because the foreign ministry was always begging him for secret rulings that would give them the authority to perform certain tasks that violated both the spirit and the letter of the law. In the past, all these requests had been rejected.

However, with three such requests currently on his desk, there was little doubt he could barter and get what he wanted.

Conti's email informed Ragno that he should expect to be gone for a week—two days to deliver the suitcase and return and five days in Washington at a suite at the Willard InterContinental Hotel. All his expenses would be paid, and he would be provided a gorgeous escort to ensure he wasn't lonely. His only responsibility, once on US soil, was to be on the Fifteenth Street NW side of the White House at precisely 2:15 p.m. and press a speed-dial number on the cell phone that would be delivered with the suitcase. It would connect him to an Italian diplomat who would take possession of what he was transporting.

Ragno wasn't one to look a gift horse in the mouth, not for $1 million. Therefore, he didn't care what was inside the suitcase. He called the minister of foreign affairs and requested a meeting, and the pair came to an agreement. After that, things moved quickly. He approved the three requests on his desk that violated a plethora of laws that a first-year law student would have recognized. At the same time his counterpart sent by messenger a large envelope that contained a diplomatic passport, an authorization to use an Italian Air Force aircraft, and a diplomatic sticker—an eight-by-three-inch laminate that bore the seal of the Ministry of State Affairs and the address of the Italian embassy in Washington.

Once he had received the package from the minister of finance, Ragno sent an encrypted message to Conti updating him. Sometime after that, the suitcase and phone arrived.

Indro Montanari was thirty-two years old and an only child. He was born in Palermo, Sicily, where his parents were killed in a car accident when he was ten years old. Since his grandparents had died one year prior to that, the court placed him into foster care. His foster parents were a salt-of-the-earth middle-income couple who also lived in Palermo, where the husband was employed as an electrical engineer specializing in designing security systems and interfacing them into computer networks. Over the years, Indro took an interest in his work and began to learn a great deal about the interrelationships between security systems, software interfaces, and computer networks. He even began reading engineering and programming books to supplement what he'd been taught, taking to the complicated manuals as readily as a duck took to water. His foster father called him a genius, although Indro never took that description seriously. However, he was anxious to make his mark in life and wasn't about to wait in line for that opportunity. Therefore, instead of employing his knowledge in engineering and computers to obtain employment, he used it to gain entry, electronic and physical, to places he wasn't invited. In the process, he became a millionaire at a young age. When he was eighteen, he ceased to be a ward of the state and said goodbye to his foster parents, telling them he had a job in Rome. The next day, their mortgage and credit cards were anonymously paid off, and $100,000 was deposited into their bank account.

Montanari's wealth and confidence grew over the next twelve years, until the day Mauro Bruno, holding two cups of espresso, entered the rare coin dealer's vault that Montanari was robbing. Of course, there was a legion of Polizia di Stato standing directly behind the chief inspector. Apparently, Montanari needed glasses—he'd touched the wrong contact on the cipher lock circuit board and set off a silent alarm. Sentenced to five years in prison, he was two years into his term when his life changed. Again, it was Bruno Mauro who was responsible. The chief inspector called him in prison and asked for the step-by-step process to get past an electronic security system; he needed to bypass an RFID system securing the vault at a home that he and Donati had broken into. Montanari shook his head in amazement because what Bruno and Donati were doing was exactly what had sent him to jail. Nevertheless, he talked Bruno through the procedures necessary to get past the embedded security protocols, helping Bruno to expose the person who had killed his father. Shortly thereafter, Montanari's sentence was commuted. The two remained friends, with Bruno referring the now-reformed thief's security firm, New Life Consulting, to what became his first and largest client—the Catholic Church. Even so, Montanari always dreaded receiving Bruno's calls because they weren't typically social. Instead, the former chief inspector primarily called when he needed something, usually something illegal.

The now-reformed thief lived in a modest two-bedroom condo in the Prati district of Rome, which was within walking distance of the Vatican. He was stirring a simmering pot of spaghetti sauce, which still had an hour to go before it was done, when his cell phone rang. Looking at the caller ID, he saw that it was Mauro Bruno.

Answering the call, Montanari said, "I'm sorry. I'm out of the country on an engagement and will be traveling in areas that have intermittent or no cell service. Therefore, I won't be able to return your call for four weeks. Goodbye." Montanari ended the call, put his phone on the counter, and went back to stirring his spaghetti sauce. Thirty minutes later, he heard a knock on his door. When he opened it, he saw a uniformed officer extending a cell phone toward him.

"Deputy Commissioner Acardi sends his regards and wondered if you'd like to take Mauro Bruno's call here or at his office?" the officer said.

Montanari took the phone without comment and walked back into the kitchen as the officer entered the residence and took a seat on the couch.

"*Pronto*?" Montanari asked, although he knew who the caller was.

"Indro, I'm glad our connection has improved," Bruno said.

"You're not a social caller, Mauro. Don't take this the wrong way, because I owe you a lot for getting me released from prison early and referring me to my current clients, but I have no desire to be your cellmate," Montanari said, turning off the power to the phone and handing it back to the waiting officer.

No sooner had Montanari done this than the officer's personal phone rang. Answering it, the officer handed it back to Montanari with a smirk on his face.

"All right, explain what you need me to do and what I'll probably go to jail for," he said.

"I need you to break into the Conti Petroleum computer system and see if you can find anything unusual. Also, let me know what they do with their cash."

"Of course. Just so I know when the arresting officer asks me, why am I breaking into this computer system?"

"Because I believe Antonio Conti is a terrorist."

"The owner of one of the country's biggest companies is a terrorist? Why?"

"For one, he tried to have Donati and me killed."

"Someone's always trying to kill the two of you, and Conti, if he was involved, would be only one in a long list of suspects. Why do you think he's the person who wants you and Donati dead?"

"Because I saw a photo of him standing beside a crate of weapons being loaded into his helicopter. I also believe that he's planning a terror attack in Italy. I need you to look inside his hard drive to see if he's planning an attack and, if so, where and when."

"That's different."

CHAPTER 7

ONAIS CHECKED INTO the Hotel Vecchio Mulino and was given a room several doors down the hall from Bruno and Donati. After dropping off her carry-on, she joined Donati in the small lounge to the side of the reception desk, where a bottle of limoncello and four glasses were sitting on the table. Twenty minutes later, Bruno entered the lounge.

"I see you two haven't lost your knack for getting into trouble when I'm not here to protect you," Donais said with a smile, standing and giving Bruno a peck on each check before she sat back down.

"If you and Messina hadn't shot those two men, Elia and I would be on stainless-steel gurneys beside Nicchi at the coroner's office."

"Do you still think it was Conti?" Donais asked.

"I have no doubt it was him, or his henchman Rotolo. Not after seeing the photo of him next to an arms crate that was about to be loaded into his helicopter," Bruno replied.

Donais gave him a questioning look.

"Sorry," Donati said. "In the excitement of almost being killed, I forgot to tell you about the photograph the bartender gave us."

"He's an arms smuggler?"

"And possibly worse," Donati replied.

"I'm curious. Did you show him a photo of the artifact?" Donais asked.

"I did. He denied knowing what it was, but his body language told me differently."

"How?"

"Because he held his breath the entire time that he looked at it," Bruno replied. "That's a classic sign that someone is holding something back or lying. Interestingly, he asked if I had the artifact, probably meaning at our hotel, since I'd just shown him an image of it on my cell phone. That's not a question I'd expect from someone who wasn't familiar with what they were being shown. Then when I said that I didn't have it, he went silent."

Donais took the square piece of silver out of her pocket and placed it on the table. "It's not jewelry, at least not something anyone with taste would wear," she said. "But I do have an idea what it might be. On the plane I was reading a book on America's NSA."

Bruno—and from the look on his face, Donati too—knew that the NSA was an obsession with Donais, who had great respect for the super-secret American spy agency and read anything she could about it.

"The unevenly spaced holes remind me of what the NSA calls a one-time pad. That's an encryption technique where two people have a one-time preshared key. It's unbreakable so long as the pad isn't reused. While this isn't an OTP," Donais said, using the acronym, "which would require the encryption/decryption key be used only once and then destroyed, it could still be a template to both encode and decode messages between two or more people."

"You'll have to explain that to me," Donati said.

"What if I sent you a letter or an email, using a set font type and size and placing the words in such a way that the letters of my hidden text appear under the holes in this piece of silver."

"So that I would compose my text using suitable words and spacing them in such a way that the letters of my hidden message appeared beneath the holes," Donati said.

"Exactly."

"How would the person deciphering the message know where to place the first hole?" Bruno asked.

"You'd have a preset symbol, number, or character that would repeat throughout the message, because the artifact has only so many holes," Donais said. "For example, I place the first hole over, let's say, a percent sign and then copy the letters or numbers under the other holes. When I reach the last hole, I repeat the process starting with the next percent sign, and so forth."

"It sounds like it would be difficult, if not impossible, to compose a message in this manner," Donati said.

"Not really. You write your message, place the required number of spaces between them, which you know from having the template, and then compose words that incorporate those letters into a message. You'd use spaces, dashes, commas, and so on to create the proper spacing. Who cares, for example, if you have two or three extra spaces between words or misspellings?"

"I think you're onto something," Bruno said.

They continued discussing this over drinks. Two hours later, Taranto Messina entered the lobby, found them, and took a seat beside Donais. Donati filled a small glass with limoncello, handed it to him, and refilled the other three glasses.

"*Salute!*" Donati said, raising his glass, a chorus repeated by the other three.

Since Bruno, Donati, and Donais had already put a large dent in the bottle of limoncello prior to Messina's arrival, Donati ordered a second while Bruno brought Messina up to date.

"It's too bad we can't look inside his hard drive to find out more about Antonio Conti and what he's up to," Donais said.

"Perhaps we can," Bruno replied. "We'll know shortly." And then he went on to explain.

Haamid Khakwani was barely five feet tall. At seventy years old, his back was stooped, and his stride had shortened so that he shuffled more than walked. Yet as he went through the courtyard of the Pakistan Academy of Sciences, the country's most respected scientific institute, where he'd long served as a fellow, every person bowed their head in respect as he passed.

Khakwani's wife and three sons had died long ago—she in her sleep and his sons in the mountains of Afghanistan when the Great Satan was pummeling the country, trying to kill Osama bin Laden. Bitter over what had happened to his offspring, and too old to fight in the field, he had approached his son's commander, Sargon Zebari, and offered his services in support of al-Qaeda. For the next seventeen years, Zebari had used him to develop sophisticated electronic devices that were incorporated into bombs that killed and maimed scores of civilians and foreign troops. However, Khakwani believed that his latest creation, a solution to a difficult problem that Zebari had given him the year before, was his greatest achievement. He prayed daily that Allah would grant him another two decades of life so that he could continue to invent ways to kill the enemies of Islam and send back planeloads of their coffins to the infidels' unholy mothers and fathers. And if this creation was as successful as he expected, that's exactly what would happen.

Sargon Zebari lived a life of fear. He never slept in the same place two nights in a row and sometimes moved between houses twice in a single day. And even though the Americans were constantly searching for him, they hadn't put the pedal to the metal and pulled out all the stops. He was no coward by any stretch of the imagination, but neither did he doubt what would occur following the terrorist attacks that he and his adopted son were about to undertake. If he was going to kill three world leaders, especially the president of the United States, and essentially make the White House and surrounding government buildings such as the US Treasury uninhabitable for a generation, then he'd better be off the grid. Otherwise, the Americans would ensure that his life expectancy was cut short. In the Middle East, off the grid meant Iran.

In preparation for what was about to come, Zebari had moved to Rasht, a city of 650,000 on the edge of the Caspian Sea and two hundred miles northwest of Tehran. The Iranian government had selected this location because there was nothing of interest there for American satellites or drones to photograph. To keep him safe, four Revolutionary Guards were assigned as bodyguards, not only because the government feared that a Shia fanatic would discover who he was and try to assassinate the al-Qaeda leader and Sunni terrorist, but also to ensure that he wouldn't do anything to inadvertently reveal his presence. The backstory that his neighbors would eventually learn, from those hired to spread the word, was that he was a retired widower with two sons and two nephews, all living in his compound. And although he was moderately well-off, having just sold his paper goods businesses in Tehran, he still hadn't gotten over the recent death of his wife and had become a recluse, which explained why he was rarely seen.

Zebari's currency in his deal with Iran, to get Iran to harbor him, was his willingness to use his network to seamlessly move men and arms into the West, an ability he'd just demonstrated with his transport of the dirty bomb. Another factor in his favor was his ability to plan and execute an attack on Western soil, something he had yet to demonstrate. That's why, unknown to his adopted son, he had decided to load the dice and direct four Iraqi fighters who'd been given Italian citizenship to conduct a parallel but separate attack.

CHAPTER 8

S AAD BACHIR, ZIAD Sadig, Rahim Yozef, and Yasin Baqir
were refugees—at least as far as Italy was concerned.
They were also members of al-Qaeda, although they
had left that part out when filling out the paperwork they
gave to Giancarlo Ragno. In their early to midtwenties, they
all shared a belief that martyrdom was their fastest way
to paradise and the rewards Allah had in store for them.
None feared death, only failure to carry out the assignment
that had been entrusted to them. Three had only the most
basic schooling. The exception was Yasin Baqir, who was the
smartest of the group and had previously been sent by Zebari
to study electrical engineering at the Pakistan Academy
of Sciences. Five years after his studies, he and his three
compatriots stepped onto an overcrowded rubber dinghy in
Sabratha, Libya. They made it only as far as international
waters before they ran out of fuel, which was the scenario of
most refugees headed to Italy from Libya because those who
sold passage knew they couldn't put enough fuel on board
for the dinghy to reach the Italian coast. Smugglers therefore
counted on the Italian navy to find and rescue the refugees
when their crafts ran out of gas. If they didn't, oh well.

The four al-Qaeda refugees were among the twenty-five men, women, and children the navy brought aboard their vessel. After being given clothing and warm food, they were transported three hundred miles to Catania, on the island of Sicily, where they asked for political asylum. For the next two months, they lived in temporary housing, during which time they were required to perform menial tasks while their paperwork was being processed. This meant working on local farms where they picked fruits and vegetables, receiving only a fraction of the wages given to nonrefugee workers.

Sixty-two days after they arrived in Catania, everyone who had been on the dinghy was sent to an Italian city that would absorb them into society—or so it was hoped. The four members of al-Qaeda, thanks to Giancarlo Ragno, were given preferential treatment and flown to Rome, where they were presented with citizenship papers. They were also, as requested by Conti, given employment at the city's sanitation department. Since the job of cleaning the municipal sewer lines wasn't exactly one that attracted many applicants, Ragno happily accommodated that request.

Baqir, in addition to being tasked by Zebari with conducting a terrorist attack on the West, separate from but parallel in timing to Conti's attack, was the lynchpin for both attacks in that he was responsible for disabling the Civitavecchia natural gas pipeline. Unless this occurred, nothing was going to happen, and years of planning would be reduced to a theoretical exercise.

Thanks to a blueprint of the port's natural gas distribution system, which had been obtained by Ragno and given to Conti, Baqir knew exactly which pipeline valves were critical to the flow of natural gas into Rome. The next step, gaining access to the LNG terminal, turned out to be only a matter of wearing his city worker's uniform and presenting an employee ID to security. The heavy metal box he was carrying when he entered the terminal, which contained an electrostatic discharge device, was inspected and presumed by the gate guard to be a maintenance device. From start to finish, it took Baqir less than a minute to fry the valves and disable the city's natural gas pipeline. The operation was on.

Massimo Albrici, Italy's minister of economic development, was at the top of the pyramid, administering a plethora of government services and providing support for local businesses in Italy. His responsibilities included not only recommending economic policies and business incentives but also setting standards for the country's telecommunications, energy and mineral resources, consumer protection, and tourism departments. Since a problem in any of these areas directly affected the public, he was constantly the butt of jokes and Twitter rants when anything went wrong.

The forty-seven-year-old gray-headed minister, who stood five feet, seven inches tall, with a trim physique, had a raging headache and was not in a good mood. He had just finished a staff meeting and was sweating profusely as he walked down the corridor from the conference room to his office. The exceptionally cold winter, along with a booming economy, had taken its toll on the city's natural gas reserves, which were at this moment nearly nonexistent.

Following the mechanical problem with the last LNG tanker headed to Civitavecchia, he had tried to get other EU nations to divert one of their LNG deliveries to Italy, but all had the same problems of low reserves and high demand. Nevertheless, he'd managed the situation to date so that no home or business had gone without gas. With the *Trochus* only hours from the LNG terminal, he should have been jubilant that the natural gas storage tanks at Civitavecchia would soon be filled. However, just minutes ago, he'd learned that there had been a major malfunction with the transmission pipes that transferred the LNG to the city when a series of valves had shorted due to an electrical overload. That meant that the system that transported gas from Civitavecchia to Rome and its environs was completely inoperative.

Albrici initially thought that finding valve replacements wouldn't be an issue, because surely other LNG terminals used similar equipment, or the manufacturer had some in stock. As it turned out, both of those assumptions were wrong. He soon discovered that the valves at the Civitavecchia terminal had been designed according to very specific engineering specs. That made them unique. The manufacturer indicated that it would take a week to produce the four replacements because some of the electrical components came from subcontractors that were scattered throughout the country. Albrici knew that he didn't have a week's supply of natural gas in storage. At best, he had two to three days. Having reached his office, he popped two Alka-Seltzer tablets into a glass of water and gulped down the liquid, hoping that it would settle his stomach.

The knock on his door startled Albrici, and one of his aides entered his office without waiting for an invitation. The man, who was clearly nervous, blurted out that he had a temporary solution to get around the broken gas distribution line. After the twenty-something-year-old presented his idea, Albrici stared at him in disbelief for a moment because his solution sounded too simple and was something Albrici himself should have thought of. Using natural gas transport vehicles to move the natural gas stranded at the port into

Rome to refill storage tanks would be a throwback to the days just after World War II. Nevertheless, it had worked then, and he believed it would work now. With his back to the wall, Albrici was ecstatic about the idea because it would get him around his only other options—running out of natural gas or rationing it. Moreover, having the gas shortage during the NATO summit would make Italy the butt of jokes throughout the EU. When that happened, he'd be out of a job. The only problem he foresaw in implementing the plan was finding enough gas transport vehicles.

Since no other option gave even a possibility of his political survival, he ordered his aide to assemble every natural gas transport vehicle within Rome at Civitavecchia and then beg, borrow, or steal whatever vehicles he could from neighboring cities. If he was lucky, Albrici just might get through this unscathed. As it would turn out, unscathed was a matter of interpretation.

Indro Montanari was a Red Bull and cannoli junkie, keeping an ample supply of both in a mini refrigerator beside his desk. He had become hooked on the creamy Italian dessert because his Sicilian grandmother had frequently made it for him when he was young. Thankfully, there were several shops in his area that sold passable imitations. His third addiction was to spaghetti sauce, which he made for himself weekly and put on nearly everything he ate, although his first choice was hot, crusty Italian bread. Yet with a metabolism that would be the envy of any dieter, the five-foot-six engineering and computer genius weighed only 130 pounds—anorexic by Italian standards. In addition to his thinness and the way he kept his black hair so short that it didn't even need to be combed, he stood in contrast to the stereotypical dapper look of most Italian men his age by dressing like an American, wearing Levi jeans, loose-fitting long-sleeved black uncollared shirts, and athletic shoes.

It took Indro Montanari nearly four hours, a dozen cannoli, and six cans of Red Bull to penetrate the Conti Petroleum computer system. He was surprised that its level of sophistication was on par with that of some of the Fortune 500 companies and government agencies he'd penetrated in his former life.

Not knowing how much time he'd have before his presence was discovered, he decided the first order of business was to download Conti's entire database. Utilizing a virtual private network proxy that hid his IP address, he copied the data to an untraceable protected server he maintained off-site. Once the transfer was complete, he altered the internal recordkeeping of the computer he'd hacked to hide the copying of information. He then exited the system.

Looking at what he'd stolen, Montanari saw that the data was divided into a series of folders, each with a generic title describing its contents. The first was titled "Financial Records with Attached Footnotes." This contained the company's balance sheet, income statement, and other financials, which showed that Conti Petroleum was extremely profitable, generating daily revenue of almost $1 million per rig and netting about half of that after expenses, which included Italy's 24 percent corporate tax. Continuing to comb through the folders, he found that the reclusive oilman regularly wired most of his company's earnings to more than two dozen numbered offshore accounts. Montanari knew he had no chance of penetrating the computer systems of these offshore repositories, which probably had firewalls as good as a nation-state.

Montanari didn't consider sending money offshore to be necessarily sinister, because Italy had a history of unstable financial institutions, and if one had the ability, keeping money in an offshore account was considered prudent. Moreover, since it was widely known that a Swiss fund was the backer for Conti's exploration and platform construction, the offshore accounts could explain how Conti was paying his investors without those distributions being reflected in the financials. Those payments were apparently recorded in a second set of books that were kept in a separate location. He believed that to be unusual, but not illegal because Conti paid taxes on his company's profits and could therefore do what he wanted with the money after that.

Opening the next folder, which was titled "Real Estate," he saw that it had information on only one asset—a house in Caprarola, which was thirty-seven miles north of Rome and 341 miles from Monopoli. Montanari had been to that town once before and liked it because it was adjacent to the woods, a nature preserve, and the Lago di Vico, a volcanic lake. What he found puzzling, however, was that a check of Caprarola's real estate records, which were in the public domain, indicated that the property was owned by a trust. He wondered why Conti had the home in the first place since he essentially lived on the oil platform, and why go to the trouble of setting up a trust for a house that was worth less than $200,000? He also asked himself who, if anyone, was living there.

Continuing to delve into the files for the next two hours, he found nothing unusual until he accessed the last folder, which was titled "The Sword of Allah." When Montanari double-clicked on it, the image of a gray globe positioned against a black background filled his computer screen.

On top of the globe was what he would later learn was a representation of the Quran, from which a rifle, a fist, and a flag emerged. Several seconds later, the symbol faded away, and a series of folders appeared. Opening one at random, he saw that the content was written in Arabic.

Using a translation program that automatically converted Arabic to Italian, Montanari saw that each of the folders bore a number. The first contained, as best he could estimate, around two hundred subfolders, each of which included a photo and the background of someone Montanari assumed to be a terrorist. He made this assumption because attached to each man's picture—there were no photos of women in any of the folders—was a glowing recommendation letter from an imam, indicating that the individual would gladly die to kill infidels and enforce the will of Allah. Each folder also provided the person's current location, with 75 percent appearing to reside in Europe, while the remainder were scattered throughout the world. The second numbered folder contained an inventory of weapons and explosives. The third gave the location of warehouses in Europe where arms and explosives had been sent. The fourth through seventh folders contained detailed engineering drawings of the Quirinal, the Hassler, the Westin Excelsior, and the St. Regis, along with various routes from these hotels to the Quirinal and back.

Montanari copied the translated data to a secure data vault, which he'd rented by using an anonymous cash card, and sent Bruno the information he needed to access that site. Once he'd finished, he went back to his stove, turned up the heat, and began stirring his spaghetti sauce.

CHAPTER 9

BRUNO, DONATI, DONAIS, and Messina were still sitting at a table in the lounge of the Hotel Vecchio Mulino, with a severely depleted bottle of limoncello between them. They were somewhere between still with the program and feeling no pain when two vehicles screeched to a halt outside the hotel. Moments later, four doors slammed shut. All stopped drinking and looked at the entrance, wondering why the vehicles' occupants were in such a hurry and who they were. That question was answered seconds later when four state police officers burst into the lobby, three of them with their handguns drawn.

Bruno, who had a perplexed look on his face, raised his hands, and the others around him followed. All had worked in or with law enforcement long enough to know that nothing good would come from arguing with three officers in their twenties who were now pointing their weapons directly at them. These three were the muscle, but the person in charge was an older man, twenty years their senior, who was standing behind them and watching. He had hazel eyes that seemed to pierce through the person he was looking at, and his black hair was combed straight back. He wore a black suit that was every bit as shiny as Bruno's from years of wear, a white shirt, and a charcoal-striped tie. His black loafers were neither scuffed nor shiny. At five feet, eleven inches tall and 250 pounds, all of which appeared to be muscle, he cut an imposing figure of authority.

After one of the three officers ordered Bruno, Donati, and Donais to stand and interlock their fingers on top of their heads, the investigators were searched, and the contents of their pockets placed on the table. The older man, who was standing behind the officers, took both sets of car keys off the table and went back outside. Ten minutes later, he returned.

Messina introduced the older man as Pietro Grosso and asked him what was going on.

"We have an arrest warrant for these three," Grosso responded.

"On what charge?"

"Charges. They're accused of selling illicit firearms, murdering two men outside the Tre Taverne, and killing Domenico Marchetti, a Taranto reporter who was about to break a story on their smuggling operation."

"That's ridiculous," Messina responded. "I killed the two men at the tavern and filed a report to that effect before I came here. As for Domenico Marchetti, Bruno and Donati were in Milan when he was killed. I know, because I saw them arrive at the Bari airport. At that time Marchetti was already at the coroner's office. Donais was also in Milan and didn't arrive in Monopoli until long after Marchetti died. Who signed the arrest order?"

"Judge Niccolo Pecora."

Messina rolled his eyes upon hearing the name. "The best judge that money can buy."

"I don't disagree with you, Gabriel, but I found a cache of illegal weapons in the trunks of their vehicles, all with the registration numbers removed. If nothing else, this requires that I take them into custody."

Messina nodded his acceptance of the inevitable and backed away.

Bruno, who'd been listening to this exchange, had the look of someone who realized that he'd been set up and was in very serious trouble.

"Place them in cuffs," Grosso said to the officers.

Thirty minutes later, Bruno, Donati, and Donais were in their cells.

Acardi stared at his phone in disbelief following the call from his nephew.

"What is it?" asked the person standing beside Acardi.

"The three investigators that I sent to investigate my brother-in-law's death have been arrested on three counts of murder and the possession of illegal weapons."

"They've been in Monopoli less than a day. How is that possible?"

"It's not." Acardi explained how the murder charges would be relatively easy to disprove, but defending against the weapons possession charges would be much harder.

"They must be getting close. Otherwise, no one would go to this much trouble to frame them."

"That's what I think. I know the judge who ordered their arrest. He's crooked and only retains his judicial standing because he's constantly shielded from removal by the minister of justice."

"Judge Niccolo Pecora?"

Acardi nodded.

"I even tried to have him removed, but unfortunately, as you said, under our system of law only the minister can do that."

"With three murder charges against them, they've been denied bail. Hopefully, that will change when I have the murder charges dismissed, however long that takes. But even then, I'm betting that the judge won't let them get past the front door of the jailhouse before he finds another charge that would throw them back in their cells—because that's obviously what he's been paid to do."

"And you can't investigate because with the NATO summit just around the corner, every person under you is committed to the security and safety of those in attendance. Bad timing."

"Or is it?" Bruno asked himself out loud.

"You'll have to explain that to me. In the meantime, perhaps I can help."

Bruno, Donati, and Donais were released from jail minutes after President Enrico Orsini signed a presidential pardon and faxed it to Pietro Grosso. Walking out of the detention facility, they were met by Messina, who was standing beside Donais's red Fiat 124 Spider and his own black Fiat 500X.

"Do we have you to thank for getting us released?" Bruno asked.

"I don't have enough clout to get a parking ticket fixed. My uncle was speaking to President Orsini when I called to notify him of your arrest. It was the president's idea to issue a presidential pardon. He followed that up with a phone call to the judge, threatening to have the military haul you out of jail if you weren't immediately released. He also threatened to give you a military escort if the judge tried to arrest the three of you again."

"Where's my rental car?" Bruno asked, looking around and not seeing the white Lancia Ypsilon.

"It's on a flatbed truck, on its way back to the rental agency in Bari. I'm afraid some of my overzealous colleagues began taking it apart, looking for anything that might have been hidden within the vehicle. Fortunately, they didn't have time to disassemble the Fiat Spider."

"Let's get back to the hotel and talk about what we're going to do next—that is, if we still have our rooms," Donati said.

"I called the hotel and confirmed that you still have them," Messina said. "Given what's happened, my uncle has asked me to stay there as well, to ensure we don't have another infraction conjured up by Judge Pecora. I also have a couple of ideas that I'd like to share."

"We can use all the help we can get, Gabriel," Donais said.

"Thank you, Lisette."

Bruno didn't know why he was unhappy to hear Donais and Messina calling each other by their first names. From the expression on Donati's face, he didn't like it either. Donais, in contrast, seemed to like being addressed as Lisette by the handsome Italian and offered him a ride to the hotel in her car. As they walked to her rental car, Messina threw the key to his Fiat 500X to Donati, who caught it in his right hand. A moment later, Bruno and Donati watched with less than thrilled looks on their faces as the red roadster sped away.

CHAPTER 10

C ONTI WAS SEETHING. The judge who'd issued the arrest warrants for Bruno, Donati, and Donais and who was paid a fortune each year to follow orders had assured him that they'd remain behind bars until the conclusion of the NATO summit. However, a presidential pardon had changed that.

"I feel like a juggler who's constantly given more balls to keep in the air," Conti told Rotolo. "The investigation of Nicchi's death, the arrival of those three investigators, and the inability to kill or even place them in jail all pose an unacceptable risk to our operation. It's the law of unintended consequences. The longer they investigate, the greater the possibility that they'll stumble onto something."

"They won't figure it out in time. They're not even on the periphery of discovering our plan."

"I wish I could share your optimism. For me, this is not just about destroying NATO—it's revenge against the organization that killed my father. They had no business interfering in a dispute that was none of their concern."

"This is where they're centering their investigation, not in Rome," said Rotolo. "They'll stay close to us, which means in Monopoli, and then read about the tragedy along with the rest of the world."

"We won't get a second opportunity because there's no telling when the summit will return to Italy," Conti said. The annual NATO meeting was normally held at the organization's headquarters in Brussels, Belgium. Over time, security there had become so tight that no amount of ingenuity could penetrate it. Therefore, al-Qaeda didn't even try. The hole in NATO's armor had appeared when it decided to have its member states begin hosting the annual summit. Five years ago, a schedule of future meetings had been published, with Italy hosting the event on the fifth year.

"They don't know anything," Rotolo insisted.

"You keep saying that. Given Bruno and Donati's reputations, I can't afford to take a chance that they'll stumble on a clue, not this close to the operation. Are they back at their hotel?"

"I sent one of my men to keep an eye on them. The last I heard, they were sitting in the lobby of the hotel."

"Pick our best fighter to join him, and make sure they have some heavy firepower. I want all three of these meddlesome insects and anyone who's with them dead within the hour. Given the arms discovered in the trunk of their cars, it'll look like someone took exception to the fact that their weapons were confiscated—either that or to not being paid. No screw-ups this time. Make sure you tell our men that if any of their targets survive, then they might as well kill themselves. Otherwise, I will."

Bruno, Donati, and Donais returned to the hotel and cleaned up before meeting Messina in the lounge. After each ordered an espresso, the bartender brought four small cups of the strong brew to their table and said that he was leaving for the night, but he'd left the espresso maker unlocked so they could help themselves.

Once he'd left, Donati, Donais, and Messina began exchanging ideas on how they could get the evidence needed to take down Conti. While they were doing this, Bruno opened and turned on his laptop to see if he'd received anything from Montanari. He could have used his cell phone, but he found it difficult to read anything on his iPhone SE, which he refused to get rid of in favor of a model with a larger screen because the phone fit easily in his pocket and snugly in his hand.

The Dell Inspiron took less than thirty seconds to pull itself together, after which Bruno accessed his corporate website and saw that he had a message from Montanari. Opening it, he followed Montanari's instructions and eventually connected to a data vault, where a summary sheet listed the general contents of what the semireformed thief had purloined from Antonio Conti's computer. Bruno told Donati and Donais what he had received, and they quickly moved behind him to get a better look at the screen.

"This proves that Conti and al-Qaeda are working together," Bruno said. "It also seems to indicate that he's planning to attack the NATO summit, given the extensive drawings of the Quirinal where the summit is being held and several hotels where I presume the world leaders are staying."

"I don't know how anyone could get near the Quirinal— even above or below it—with the president of the United States in attendance," Donais said. "American security is always over the top. Nevertheless, we need to get this information to Acardi as quickly as possible."

Bruno agreed and forwarded Montanari's email to Acardi. Messina pulled his cell phone from his pocket and said that he'd give his uncle a heads-up on what was being sent. Just as he was about to touch the screen to dial Acardi, a barrage of bullets disintegrated the lounge's large plate glass window. Messina and Donais, who were standing at the time, were hit and went down hard. Donati was luckier because he was leaning over and looking at Bruno's computer screen when one bullet grazed his jacket and another two shattered the right armrest of his chair beside him. Donati didn't have time for conscious thought. His reflexes and instincts as a former state police officer took over, and he dove to the floor just as a cascade of bullets raked the spot where he'd stood a moment earlier. Bruno, with a similar survival reflex, dove to the floor at approximately the same time. Messina was lying on his stomach several feet away, with several exit wounds visible in his back. The fact that his eyes were open and his mouth was agape told Bruno that he was dead. Donais wasn't moving either, but she was groaning. It was apparent that she'd been hit, but just how seriously was still a mystery.

As the barrage continued, Bruno and Donati crawled closer to the wall, which formed the exterior of the building and was constructed of brick to a height of three feet, over which the window had once stood. As they crawled, Donati grabbed Donais and dragged her with him while Bruno did the same with Messina's body, so that Acardi would at least be able to see his nephew relatively intact. Tucking Messina's body against the wall, Bruno saw that the Taranto officer had a shoulder holster containing a 9 mm Beretta as well as an ankle holster holding a 9 mm Beretta Nano, previously hidden by the leg of his trousers and now exposed from his body being dragged. Bruno pulled both out, handing the larger handgun to Donati while he took the Nano.

After the gunfire stopped, it didn't take more than a few seconds for the first gunman to come through the opening where the front door had once been, and which had now been reduced to kindling. As he walked, he had all the confidence of a hunter approaching his trophy kill—which was to say he assumed that everyone was dead, and therefore he was careless. He was holding his assault rifle loosely at his side, and that inattentiveness cost him his life as Bruno and Donati simultaneously put bullets into his head. The trailing gunman was a different story. Hearing gunshots that clearly didn't belong to his partner, he emptied a full clip into every conceivable space in front of him as he entered the lobby. However, since Bruno and Donati were prone on the floor to the man's right, this cavalcade of bullets ripped harmlessly through the room. As the second gunman began to reload, he also took two to the head.

While Donati crawled out the front door to see if anyone else was in line to try to kill them, Bruno yelled to the registration clerk and told him that it was clear. A moment later, a man in his midsixties poked his head out of the back room and said that he'd called for the police at the first sound of gunfire. Looking at Donais and Messina lying on the floor, he said he'd also call for an ambulance and ran back into his office.

Donati returned and had just knelt next to Donais when she opened her eyes. She tried to sit up, and he told her to stay still and asked where it hurt. When she pointed to her ribs, he knelt and gently touched the area, discovering that she was wearing a bulletproof vest.

"I think I broke a couple of ribs," Donais said, grimacing in pain as Donati helped her first to a sitting position and then to her feet.

In the process, Donais saw Messina's body. The look on her face and the tears that followed tore at Bruno and Donati. She told them that Messina had insisted she wear his vest until he picked up another at the station in the morning. "If he hadn't done that," she said, "I'd be dead instead of him."

With the sound of sirens approaching the hotel, Bruno dug his cell phone out of his pocket. He phoned Acardi and told him that his nephew had been killed, emphasizing that he'd died a hero and that those who'd murdered him were dead—a bittersweet reprisal for the death of too many law enforcement officers.

Dante Acardi arrived at the Bari Karol Wojtyła Airport at 5:30 a.m., having made the three-hundred-plus-mile trip from Rome by military helicopter. He was met by a Monopoli police officer who saluted and expressed his condolences. Trying to appear stoic and holding back his tears, except for a single drop that got away and fell down his right cheek, Acardi was handed the key to the police cruiser. After getting into the vehicle and starting the engine, he saw that the route to the hospital was displayed on the vehicle's navigation screen.

When Acardi arrived at the emergency room of the San Giacomo Hospital in Monopoli, his older sister and her husband, the Messinas, and their sister Lia Nicchi greeted him with tears and hugs.

Gabriel Messina's body was on a bed in a private room on the first floor of the hospital. When Messina's family entered the room, they found Bruno, Donati, and Donais sitting in chairs around the bed, all with sullen looks on their faces. The room was silent as the parents approached their son's body and, for the next ten minutes, grieved.

From the look on Acardi's face, it seemed that he was having a hard time holding it together. He motioned for Bruno, Donati, and Donais to follow him out into the hall.

"It's my fault he's dead," Donais said to Acardi. "If he hadn't given me his bulletproof vest, he'd still be alive."

"If you want to place the blame where it belongs, try the two men with automatic weapons who were there to kill the four of you. They're responsible for his death, not you. My nephew did what any police officer would do to protect the innocent. I'll grieve for him later, but for now, considering what you sent me, I believe a great many people are in danger."

All nodded in agreement.

"I looked at what you sent while I was en route here and trying to avoid reality, if only for a short time. I know what Montanari did for you and Donati in Paris, and even though his name wasn't on anything I received, his digital fingerprints, so to speak, were."

"A solid observation," Bruno confirmed.

"The translated folders prove that Conti is a closet terrorist. The evidence also indicates that he's planning to target the NATO summit somehow. However, we're in the dark as to exactly how. Although I don't dispute what I've been given, you've put me in a quandary. Since this information wasn't legally obtained, I can't very well use this as a basis to arrest him. Hacking a computer is a crime that legally excludes the information obtained from being used in a court of law. Therefore, to protect Montanari and the three of you, no one can find out how I received these folders. Moreover, Conti is one of the most respected people in the country. None of my superiors will do anything without proof that will stand up in a court of law. Anything short of that would be political suicide—at least in their way of thinking."

"There must be a way," Bruno stated.

Acardi stepped closer to the three investigators and looked Bruno in the eye. "There is. If I leave his name out of it and say that I received these folders anonymously, there are two government agencies that can act on this information."

"And that's what you did?" Bruno asked.

"It'll be our secret."

"Who did you send the folders to?" Donati asked.

"I forwarded them to both the Agency for External Information and Security and the Agency for Internal Information and Security."

"I've worked with each before," Bruno said. "They'll get the job done."

Donais said that she wasn't familiar with either.

"The AISE and the AISI are the Italian equivalent of America's CIA and FBI," said Acardi. "I'm working with both on the Quirinal's security. Two hundred folders of men who have letters from their imams indicating their willingness to kill infidels will keep the agencies very busy."

"Do you believe that Conti can penetrate your security and get at the NATO representatives?" Bruno asked.

"Not one of the security specialists or details from the twenty-nine member nations in attendance believes that the protection we have in place at VIP hotels, the Quirinal, and the motorcade routes is penetrable." Acardi then went on to explain that in addition to Italian security, the three heads of state would have rings of their own security detail surrounding them at all times, and since vehicles weren't allowed within two blocks of the summit, suicide bombers weren't a consideration.

"What about a rogue pilot diving a plane into the Quirinal?" Donais asked.

"Neither an air attack nor a subterranean incursion would go anywhere." Acardi then explained the extensive security measures in place, including a ten-mile-diameter no-fly zone around the Quirinal, helicopter patrols within this restricted airspace, and the General Electric M134 miniguns systems that had been installed in the subterranean areas.

"Something's going to happen," Bruno said. "If Conti has been planning an attack, he knows there will be extensive security, and if he's still moving forward—which by all indications he's doing—it's because he's found a chink in the armor."

"I've been working on the development and implementation of security protocols for this summit, alongside twenty-nine world-class security organizations, for the past year," said Acardi. "If there's a hole in our plan, the best of the best would have noticed it. However, I can't afford to take anything for granted. Sometimes planners can't see the forest for the trees. That's why I'm going to take the three of you with me to Rome, so that you can look at our security and find that chink in our armor, if it exists."

"That doesn't give us much time since the conference starts tomorrow," Bruno said.

"It starts tonight. There's a reception at six, followed by a formal dinner at eight. Tomorrow, all three heads of state will address the summit and depart the Ciampino airport later that day. Diplomats, military officers, and other functionaries will stay and document and implement what's been agreed to—or at least that's the agenda that's been given to me."

"Who's the first to arrive?" Donati asked.

"The president of the United States. He lands in a little more than three hours, which means we need to get moving if we're going to get you to Rome before him."

CHAPTER 11

AIR FORCE ONE landed at the Ciampino airport in Rome at 10:00 a.m., exactly as scheduled. Two weeks prior to its arrival, advance teams from the Secret Service had begun implementing presidential security protocols, culminating with the previous day's arrival of two C-17 Globemaster III transport aircraft. These carried two VH-3D Sea King helicopters, referred to as Marine One when occupied by the president; two presidential limousines; a small fleet of SUVs; an ambulance; a mobile command and control vehicle; fuel for Air Force One; and an electronic countermeasures Suburban, which was designed to counter an attack from projectiles such as IEDs, rocket-propelled grenades, and antitank missiles.

The president was greeted by Italian president Enrico Orsini, and after the exchange of pleasantries, POTUS walked to the first of two presidential limousines, with the other being used as a decoy. Both vehicles were nicknamed The Beast. It took the presidential caravan fifteen minutes to make the eleven-and-a-half-mile journey to the Hotel Hassler, which was located at the top of the Spanish Steps and a half mile from the Quirinal. President Ballinger then proceeded to the Presidential Suite San Pietro on the sixth floor. Although not as large or grand as the Penthouse Villa Medici Suite on the seventh floor or the Hassler Penthouse Suite on the eighth, which were occupied by both the Secret Service and senior staff, the president's quarters were more secure. Both of the other suites had large glass windows that, although offering spectacular views of Rome, would make the president an easy target for a sniper.

Two hours after the arrival of Air Force One, the Konrad Adenauer, an Airbus A340-313 VIP aircraft named after a German statesman, landed at the Ciampino airport. There the chancellor of Germany was greeted by the Italian minister of foreign affairs and escorted to her armored Mercedes-Benz S600, bearing license plate 0–1. The motorcade then proceeded to the St. Regis Hotel, which was a mile from the Quirinal.

The last head of state to arrive was the prime minister of Great Britain, whose RAF Voyager A330 aircraft landed at 2:00 p.m. She also was greeted by the Italian minister of foreign affairs and was escorted to a modified Bentley Arnage, three feet longer than the commercial version of this vehicle. The motorcade then proceeded to the Westin Excelsior Hotel, located 1.4 miles from the Quirinal.

Later that evening, beginning at 6:00 p.m., representatives from all twenty-nine member states would gather at the Quirinal, with the three heads of state arriving an hour later. Each country's security details believed they were prepared for whatever threat someone could conjure. They were wrong.

The Italian Air Force aircraft landed at the Washington Dulles International Airport thirty minutes ahead of its scheduled arrival time and taxied to the executive terminal, where Ragno disembarked with his suitcase and a modest carry-on bag. He'd gotten a fair amount of sleep on the flight thanks to the copious amount of Prosecco that he'd consumed, but he was still jet-lagged as he stepped onto the tarmac. The nine-and-a-half-hour flight also had taken a toll on his body. His head was pounding from too much Prosecco and not enough water to offset the loss of water from his system, his legs were shaky and cramping from sitting for so long, and his neck was stiff from sleeping in an awkward position.

Limping as he entered the executive terminal building, Ragno approached the single customs station and presented his diplomatic passport to the immigration official behind the glass partition. The officer maintained a neutral expression that would have been the envy of any poker player as he hit the keys on his computer keyboard. Twenty seconds later, he stamped Ragno's passport and directed him to the electronic screening station, which was cordoned off from the terminal exit by a thick nylon rope. The flow of adrenaline in Ragno's body immediately surged because Conti had told him that under no circumstances could the suitcase he was carrying be inspected or electronically screened. But as Ragno approached, the officer at that station saw the diplomatic sticker on his suitcase and took his passport to check his diplomatic status. Once this information was verified, the security officer pulled aside the stanchion securing the nylon rope and motioned him past the electronic screening station.

Exiting the terminal, Ragno saw a slender man in his midthirties holding a placard with his name on it and followed him to a black stretch limousine. He looked at his watch and saw that he had quite a bit of time, even considering the hour it would take to reach his hotel, before he was to hand over the suitcase at 2:15 p.m. He reached into his pocket and pulled out the phone that Conti had sent him. He was about to press the preset number that would connect him with whomever he was supposed to meet, to ask if he could deliver the package earlier, when his personal cell phone rang. He removed it from his other pocket and saw that there was no caller ID.

"*Pronto*?"

"Giancarlo," the caller said.

Ragno instantly recognized Conti's voice.

"You've done well. The fact that I'm speaking to you means that everything has gone as planned. Thank you."

"Since I'm in Washington ahead of schedule, I was thinking of making arrangements to deliver the package early."

"The person you're delivering this information to is extremely busy," Conti responded in a voice that did little to conceal his irritation. "Under no circumstances are you to contact him earlier than planned."

"Understood," Ragno replied defensively, indicating that he'd adhere to the original schedule.

"Wonderful. In any event, you won't have any spare time before your 2:15 p.m. delivery."

"Why is that? Is there something else you want me to do?"

"You'll see. Goodbye, Giancarlo."

The ride into Washington was faster than expected. Forty minutes after leaving Dulles, he arrived at the Willard InterContinental Hotel, entered the lobby, presented his passport to the registration clerk, and received the entry card to his suite. The clerk remarked that all his expenses were being covered by a company that Ragno had never heard of but that he assumed was a shell corporation owned by Conti.

Ragno was directed to the Willard Suite, a 720-square-foot room with views of the Washington Monument and Pennsylvania Avenue. He could only marvel at the grandeur of the elegantly decorated room he stepped into. However, what intrigued him the most was the curvaceous eighteen-year-old blonde standing at the entrance to the bedroom, wearing a negligee that left nothing to the imagination.

"Mr. Conti wanted me to welcome you to the United States in a manner you'd always remember," she said, seductively walking toward him. "I was told you have a suitcase to deliver at two fifteen this afternoon but," she said with a mischievous look on her face, "that's more than two hours away. Until then, I have something naughty planned that will make that time fly by." She took him by the arm and led him into the bedroom. And she was good to her word.

At 6:30 p.m. the drivers behind the wheels of the fifty-two LNG carrier trucks that were waiting to receive their cargo were notified that the transfer of natural gas to their vehicles would soon begin. In the plan that Albrici and his team had put together, the carriers would deliver their fuel to the city's storage tanks in a defined pecking order of ten tiers, a pecking order that the minister of economic development had kept close to his vest to avoid the discord that would naturally ensue from those who were prioritized lower on the ladder than others. Hospitals, fire and police stations, and other entities vital to welfare, safety, and national security came first. Hotels, since tourism was critical to the economy, and government offices were generally second-tier recipients. However, the Quirinal and the hotels in which the world leaders and NATO representatives would be staying were included in the first tier under the banner of national security.

Saad Bachir, Ziad Sadig, Rahim Yozef, and Yasin Baqir were in the first four ST-16300 LNG transport trailers, with Sargon Zebari's men in the sixth and seventh positions. All were only peripherally familiar with one another, having been instructed that fraternization would lead to their discovery. The six vehicles that they were driving were identical tri-axle trailers, on each one of which rested a horizonal vacuum-insulated inner tank surrounded by a thin-gauge carbon and stainless steel outer shell. Each vehicle was fifty-three feet long, eight feet, six inches wide, and twelve feet, ten inches high with a storage capacity of 50,000 pounds and the ability to off-load what it transported at three hundred gallons or 1,050 pounds, per minute.

For the past year, all eight men, in addition to being employed at the sanitation department, had held part-time jobs driving for the largest gas transport company in Rome, working there three days a week thanks to a generous bribe. Since the trucking company's owner had a reputation for paying his employees well, he thought that the bribe paid by the workers' family was to ensure that they would eventually receive full-time employment. That would lead to financial security, marriage, and ability to raise a family. This wasn't an uncommon occurrence in Europe, and the owner accepted the bribe as a normal course of progression for an individual's promotion within his company. However, later he would realize that his greed had overridden common sense, which should have led him to question why the last names of these men were all different and why they bore no family resemblance to one another, rarely socialized with each other, and were nearly the same age.

Once the trucks received their cargo of natural gas, it was only a fifty-mile drive from Civitavecchia to Rome. That meant that in less than two hours, Italy's presidential palace would be reduced to a pile of rubble, the White House and the most important buildings in the US government would be made radioactive and unusable for decades, and four nations would lose their leaders.

CHAPTER 12

T HE ITALIAN ARMY helicopter set down at the Quirinal with military precision. Bruno, Donati, and Donais followed Acardi out of the aircraft.

Once they were clear of the rotor noise, Acardi stopped and turned to the three investigators. "At 6:00 p.m., three hours from now, dignitaries from NATO's twenty-nine member countries will begin to arrive. Before then, I'll need your initial take on security."

"I'd like to start by looking at the area beneath the palace. I believe that's the most likely spot for an attack," Bruno said, "because I don't think that anyone will have much success penetrating the two-block perimeter and the numerous security staff around the palace. I also don't believe an aerial assault is likely because, as you told me on the flight here, three military helicopters are on constant patrol within the ten-mile no-fly zone. I assume that means there's a system in place that authenticates the friendlies, discerning them from the bad guys?"

"There is," Acardi confirmed. "It's a NATO Mark XII identification friend or foe, or IFF, device that transmits an encoded pulse that identifies friendlies. Without it, our helicopter wouldn't have gotten within sight of the palace.

The subterranean area you want to inspect is referred to as the utility corridor, and it runs across the entire palace grounds. I'll get someone to escort you there." The deputy commissioner asked one of the three military officers approaching them to take Bruno, Donati, and Donais into the utility corridor and give them unfettered access to anything else they wanted to see.

The man crisply saluted Acardi upon receiving this order and escorted his charges to a hardened steel door at the northwest end of the palace grounds, where he disarmed a cipher lock. Descending two flights of steel stairs, which must have dated back at least a century, they entered an empty concrete-floored room.

"The entrance to the utility corridor is through this door. I suggest you listen closely, because this is important," the officer said. "This utility corridor and the areas below the three hotels where the heads of state will be staying are military kill zones that have M134 miniguns mounted in the ceiling next to high-resolution cameras. While in these zones, you'll be under constant visual surveillance by the off-site army personnel. I'll notify the control center that you're inspecting the utility corridor, so there'll be no misunderstanding. But don't do anything radical."

He didn't define radical, but everyone got the point.

The military officer then called the security office on his cell phone and authorized the presence of three civilians in the utility corridor. Afterward, he walked several paces to his right and threw a large lever that had the word "Lighting" printed over it. "Right through that door," he said, pointing straight ahead of him. "Call me when you return to the surface and I'll escort you wherever you want to go. Here's my number," he said, writing it on a piece of paper that he tore from a notepad in his pocket and handing it to Bruno. "Security is tight, and I don't want our next meeting to be in the hospital or the morgue."

Once the officer left, Bruno turned to Donati. "How old is the Quirinal?"

"I don't know exactly," said Donati, "but something has always been on this hill, if I remember my history, since the seventh century BC. The palace above us was built by Pope Gregory XIII in the late sixteenth century and expanded over the years."

"Good to know we're entering a four-centuries-old sewer," Bruno replied. He opened the heavy steel door a sliver and sniffed. "No odor. Let's see what we're dealing with."

Pulling the door open the remainder of the way, the three investigators looked down the vast corridor before them.

"Not exactly what I expected," Donais said, seeing a pristinely clean utility corridor that was well lit by sodium vapor lighting. Running along either side were pipes and conduits wrapped in metal sheathing and labeled as cable, telecommunications, electrical, gas, steam, water, or sewer. Above them was an M134 minigun with a security camera next to it.

"Whatever Conti or anyone else is planning, it's not going to happen here," Bruno said, pointing to the minigun and camera.

"What's the metal wrapping around these pipes?" Donais asked.

"My guess," Bruno answered, "is it's low-voltage wiring that trips a circuit if someone cuts into it. That way no one can insert something in the water supply, for example."

Donati nodded, indicating that Bruno's explanation made sense.

"These seem to be only the main utility and sewer lines," Donais said, pointing to the conduits and pipes. "But in a million-plus-square-foot building, there's got to be quite a few splinter pipes within the palace that connect to these. Outside the Quirinal, they must merge with common city lines. That brings up the very real possibility that someone beyond the security perimeter could insert and send something down one of these pipes or conduits."

"By something, do you mean a missile?" Donati asked.

"That would take the miniguns out of play," Bruno said. "Another possibility is that someone wearing an oxygen tank could enter the sewage line and insert explosives with a timer directly under the palace. The pipe is definitely big enough."

As they continued walking, they saw two other miniguns and accompanying security cameras. Fifty yards beyond the last one, a heavy steel grate with a cipher lock sealed the end of the utility corridor. Just beyond the grate was an access ladder, its rungs embedded into the concrete walls, leading up to what Bruno assumed to be a manhole.

"Someone could take a torch to this grate and enter the utility corridor," Bruno said. "But I think that the miniguns would end their plan before it got started."

Donati and Donais said that they agreed.

"Again, that leaves the sewer pipe beyond this grate as the most likely point of entry," said Bruno. "Let's go back and look at the engineering drawings and see how someone could gain entry to it." With that, Bruno did an about-face and headed back, followed closely by Donati and Donais.

Acardi entered the small conference room in the Quirinal and found Bruno, Donati, and Donais seated. Taking the empty chair at the head of the rectangular table, he removed four cell phones from his jacket and pants pockets and laid them side by side on the table.

When Acardi saw the questioning looks from those around him, he explained. "This one is my Polizia di Stato phone," he said, placing a hand on the cell phone to the left. "This one," he continued, moving his hand to the next phone, "has a number that's only known by the security details of the three heads of state. The third has a number that's only been given to the security details of the other twenty-six nations in attendance. The fourth is my personal cell."

"Did anything come from the folders on Conti's computer?" Bruno asked.

"The AISI said that every person listed is an immigrant who quickly became an Italian citizen. They were inexplicably granted that privilege by the minister of justice, who moved them to the head of the line, shortcutting established procedures. I'd like to take them all in for questioning. However, as citizens they have the same rights as you and I. Therefore, I need a reason to bring them in. Quick citizenship isn't a reason. I also can't point to the fact that my information came from an illegal hack of Antonio Conti. If that were known, the four of us would be arrested instead of him."

During their conversation two of Acardi's cell phones vibrated, with the caller's names displayed on the screen. Each time, he apparently decided that he could return the call and let it go to voice mail.

Bruno acknowledged the predicament that Acardi was in and said that they'd have to find another way to get him the proof he needed. He then gave Acardi a summary of their observations, concluding with a request to examine a diagram of the sewer system.

The same two cell phones vibrated again.

"You'll have that info within fifteen minutes. I have to get moving. What else do you need?"

"That's all I can think of at the moment," Bruno confessed.

Upon hearing this, Acardi rose from his chair, picked up his cell phones, and put three of them back in his pockets, holding the phone reserved for the Polizia di Stato in his right hand.

"There is one more thing," Bruno said, putting his index finger up to indicate that he had remembered something else. "Is seeing the forest for the trees the only reason we're here?"

"If you want me to be frank, you and your two partners are a giant magnet for trouble. Look what happened in Milan and Paris. Nevertheless, in the end you took down Duke Rodolfo Rizzo, who was responsible for a score of murders, and his son, who left a similar trail of carnage across Paris. Now in the last day, you've had two attempts on your lives, you've been responsible for four dead bodies, and you were arrested for illegal possession of firearms—all before you even went to bed in Monopoli. Therefore, my magnet theory holds. If anyone is planning an attack, you'll be in the middle of it and hopefully resolve the situation without getting yourselves killed."

"That's comforting," Bruno said, lacking sincerity. "Can you at least issue us weapons?"

The cell phone in Acardi's hand vibrated, followed by two others in his pockets. "I'll send them with the diagram. Try not to get killed. It seems my sister has taken a liking to you."

The same officer who had escorted Bruno, Donati, and Donais to the utility corridor entered the conference room twenty minutes later and handed each of the three investigators a 9 mm Beretta 92S handgun. Accompanying him was a heavyset man in his midforties who carried a rolled-up blueprint in his right hand. He introduced himself as Eriberto DeRosa, the Quirinal's director of engineering.

Unrolling the large rectangular piece of paper on the conference table, DeRosa placed his car keys and his cell phone on two of the corners to anchor it down, while the officer did the same for the remaining corners. DeRosa then began to explain the Quirinal's sewer system.

"The Quirinal sits atop the highest hill in Rome. Therefore, the sewage system relies on gravity instead of lift stations or pumps to move the solids and effluent along. At intervals there are vertical concrete pipes called manholes, which connect the main sewer line to the surface," DeRosa said, pointing to several manholes on the blueprint.

"And smaller lines within the building discharge into the main pipe?" Bruno asked.

"That's correct. They're referred to as laterals. As you can see," DeRosa said, putting a finger on a small line on the drawing, "the Quirinal has five laterals that connect to the main trunk." He went on to explain that the sewer line from the Quirinal continued past the security grate they'd seen and entered an interceptor, which received multiple trunks.

"Can someone gain access to the palace by going down a manhole and entering the interceptor?" Bruno asked. "The pipe I saw in the utility corridor seems big enough."

DeRosa told them that although the Quirinal's trunk line was larger than a typical sewer pipe because it also handled stormwater management and therefore could easily accommodate one or more people, there were two safeguards that prevented someone from entering and gaining access to the palace or its grounds. "First," the director of engineering explained, "all manhole covers within the footprint of the palace and for a two-block radius beyond are welded shut. Second, there are four sets of vertical bars embedded within the sewer pipe that prevent entry. The first two are located outside the footprint of the palace grounds, and the second two within." DeRosa pointed to their locations on the diagram. "Each is strong enough to stop a significant projectile."

"Like a missile?" Donais asked.

"Within reason. Let's say a projectile that's small enough to fit through a manhole."

"Can these bars be cut?" Donati asked.

"Each bar is two inches thick and made from chromium alloy. No one is cutting through even one of them unless they have a lot of time. However, let's say that our intruder has the time and cuts deeply into a bar. Are you familiar with Tootsie Roll Pops?"

Bruno, Donati, and Donais said that they were and gave each other looks that said they all wondered what DeRosa was getting at.

"If our intruder cuts halfway through the chromium bar, he'll hit a high-voltage line that will instantly electrocute him. It will also set off an alarm. No one is entering the Quirinal through the sewage system—that, I promise you."

Once the officer and DeRosa had left, Bruno looked at Donati and Donais. "The Quirinal is a fortress," Bruno said. "That means we have exactly ninety minutes to find out what Conti already knows—how to penetrate the impenetrable."

CHAPTER 13

GIANCARLO RAGNO HAD often heard the expression "weak-kneed," but before today he'd never experienced it. He was wobbly and unsteady as he pulled the suitcase through the lobby, ten minutes behind schedule because he'd stopped in the hotel's jewelry store and picked up a gold necklace for the young lady who had so expertly brought him back to his twenties and rung his bell twice. He'd also stopped at the gift shop to buy a bottle of aspirin, hoping it would thin his blood enough to prevent cardiac arrest during his next session with the overachiever he'd just been with.

As he exited the hotel, he thought about taking a taxi to the White House, even though it was a short distance, so that he could get back on schedule. However, the taxi queue outside the hotel was ten people long. Patting the cell phone in his pocket to double-check that he had it on him, he decided to walk. In Italy being ten minutes late was considered arriving early. Since the person he was meeting also was Italian, he wasn't concerned about this small delay. He'd be punctual by Italian standards.

The Willard, which was on Pennsylvania Avenue between Fourteenth Street NW and Fifteenth Street NW, was an

A-Rod home run away from the area outside the White House where Ragno was to deliver the suitcase. However, his plan to arrive just ten minutes late flew out the window when a large group of students disembarked from four school buses directly ahead of him. This made walking on the sidewalk akin to standing in line for a main attraction at Disney World. He was in the pedestrian equivalent of carmageddon.

The fifty-three-mile ride from Civitavecchia to the center of Rome normally took around two hours because traffic in and around the city was always a mess. Today, however, because of the number of trucks carrying natural gas from the port to the city and the need to expedite the deliveries, Albrici had ordered the police to cordon off a lane from Civitavecchia to the center of Rome. Thus, the travel time for the carrier trucks was reduced to under an hour, while everyone else's increased to three.

It was 7:50 p.m. when Bachir and Yozef's trucks pulled up beside a manhole three blocks from the southern security perimeter of the Quirinal. Because this street was a narrow one-way thoroughfare, parking a vehicle on either side of the manhole effectively blocked traffic. While Yozef placed red maintenance cones twenty yards behind the two vehicles, which effectively rerouted the snail-paced traffic down similarly narrow side streets, Bachir erected a waist-high yellow canvas barrier around three sides of the manhole, removed the cover, and took two 3500-lumen LED lights from his truck down into the sewer. Since they were five blocks from the Quirinal, there was no security in the area, and the manhole covers were unwelded.

Meanwhile, Yozef unlatched the large plastic hoses from the side of each truck and connected them to their LNG flow nozzles before shoving the other ends into the manhole. He then returned to the cab of his carrier and retrieved two fans, a small Honda generator, two fifty-foot extension cords, and a speargun. After connecting the fans to the extension cords and the generator, and then attaching to a spear the specially engineered filament that Haamid Khakwani had designed, he slung the speargun over his shoulder and descended into the manhole carrying both fans in his left hand while holding onto the rungs with his right, careful not to tangle or break the filament as he descended.

Bachir had just finished squeezing the plastic hoses between the bars of the security grate when Yozef arrived. Together they secured the fans below the hoses, using their belts as cinches and directing the airflow down the sewer pipe and toward the Quirinal. Bachir then took the speargun from Yozef and sent the spear with the attached filament thirty feet into the sewer pipe. It was 8:05 p.m. when Yozef opened the valves that allowed natural gas to pour into the two plastic pipes.

As Yozef was doing this, he saw a police officer, a tall man in his midforties, park next to the maintenance cones and get out of his vehicle. He expected the officer to ask what he was doing pumping gas into a manhole, but instead he removed a yellow vest from his trunk and put it on as he walked into the street. There the officer began directing traffic and cajoling drivers to speed it up. Yozef smiled at their good fortune.

When the trucks' gauges indicated that two-thirds of the vehicles' gas had been pumped into the sewer line, Yozef yelled down to Bachir and gave him the update. It was 8:08 p.m. He still couldn't plug the ignition filament into the generator because the sewer wasn't near the proper air-to-gas ratio, which was between 5 and 15 percent. According to

Khakwani's calculations, given the diameter of the sewer line and the fact that the Quirinal was five blocks away, 95 percent of the gas in both carrier trucks had to be off-loaded. Since the filament's temperature was 1,004 degrees, the ignition point for LNG, the explosion would occur as soon as that air-to-gas ratio was reached. Khakwani had cautioned against plugging the filament in early because it had a life of only a few minutes. Therefore, Yozef needed to make sure that they had at least 90 percent of their gas into the sewer line before then.

It was 8.7 miles from the Quirinal to the NATO Defense College, or NDC as it was commonly called. Zebari's two carrier trucks were beside manhole covers on opposite sides of the NDC and were following the same procedures as Conti's men. The college, where ninety NATO officers with the rank of colonel or lieutenant colonel were domiciled, was outside the summit's security perimeters. And since essentially every officer in Rome's Polizia di Stato all the way down to meter maids had been assigned to protect the heads of state and NATO representatives, law enforcement in the area was nonexistent.

At 8:09 p.m. they began pumping LNG into the sewer system running beneath the NDC.

Bruno and his partners were impressed by the Quirinal's subterranean security. They therefore decided, since the formal dinner at the palace was in process, to look at the air defenses to see if a low-flying aircraft or drone could get past the roving helicopter patrols. The officer who had escorted them to the utility corridor now explained the Quirinal's air defense system in more detail than Acardi's previous overview.

"In regard to drones, the Quirinal has a very sophisticated drone-jamming system—the same type installed on top of the hotels where the heads of state are staying. These systems send out a pulse that destroys the electronics on a trespassing drone, causing it to drop from the sky."

"What about a jet aircraft bent on a suicide run? Couldn't it dart past the helicopters, flying low to the ground so that it was all but undetectable on radar, and crash into the palace?" Bruno asked.

"Not with the LPWS system."

"Help me out here," Donati said.

"Sorry. That's military-speak for Land Phalanx Weapon System. Do you see the two large barrel-shaped radomes mounted on those forty-foot-high steel platforms on either side of the courtyard?"

The three investigators said that they did.

"That's the LPWS. What you can't see from here is the radar-guided 20 mm Vulcan cannon mounted on a swivel base. This system is fully automated and capable of shooting down short-range missiles, rockets, artillery fire, drones, and low-flying aircraft. Without an encoded IFF signal, an aircraft would be reduced to aluminum scrap within seconds."

"That's impressive," Bruno acknowledged. "Is it possible to get a look at the surrounding area from a helicopter? I think it might give us a better sense of perspective."

The officer replied that he had been ordered to give them any support that they requested, and he turned to lead them to the helipad.

On the way, Donati spoke softly so that only Bruno and Donais could hear him. "The palace grounds, subterranean area, and airspace above it seem very secure. It's hard to imagine how something could have been overlooked, especially with the American, British, and German security services involved since their heads of state are here."

"And yet," Bruno said in a low voice, "I still believe that something's going to happen. Anyone planning an attack on the NATO summit would expect extensive security, such as the systems we were just told about, and must believe they can penetrate it. The question is, where did they find the chink in the armor?"

Bending down as they approached the entry door, they boarded the helicopter and strapped themselves in. The aircraft took off and headed south, leveling off at one thousand feet and maintaining that altitude. Less than a minute later, Bruno spoke into his headset mic. "Go back about a hundred yards. I want to take a closer look at something."

The pilot immediately complied and made a 360-degree turn.

"Hover over the police car with the flashing lights," Bruno instructed, "and shine the aircraft's spotlight on those two tanker trucks."

The pilot immediately complied.

"Why are they off-loading gas into a manhole and thus the sewer system?" Bruno asked. "One spark and ..."

Bruno didn't need to finish the sentence. He knew from the looks of understanding on Donati and Donais's faces that they'd come to the same conclusion: the subterranean security was designed to be effective against a person or an object, but not against gas.

"Set us down now!" Bruno screamed into his mic.

The pilot took one look at the area below and shook his head as he spoke. "These streets are too narrow. The diameter of the helicopter's blades makes it impossible to land anywhere around here."

Bruno briefly considered calling Acardi, but one look at the hoses going into the manhole told him that anyone Acardi might send would never arrive in time. "Hover over the rooftop patio to your right," Bruno ordered, before turning to Donati and Donais. "Let's get ready to jump."

All three moved toward the aircraft door.

No sooner had the pilot brought the helicopter into a hover six feet over the rooftop patio than Bruno yelled, "Now!"

The three investigators jumped, all landing on their feet before their momentum carried them head over heels across the deck. As the pilot increased altitude and hovered at a distance, they got to their feet and raced across the patio. Bruno flung open the sliding glass door into the penthouse apartment, and they ran past the two startled residents, who'd been standing in front of their floor-to-ceiling windows, watching the trio leap from the helicopter. The investigators ran through the apartment and out into the hallway. The elevator's indicator showed that it was on the first floor, so they opened the stairway exit and streaked down six flights of stairs to the street level.

Breathing heavily from the descent and the adrenaline rush, Bruno opened the outside door and was met with a barrage of automatic fire. Fortunately, they were shielded by the steel entry door until they could dive behind the decorative concrete planter box in front of them. It was 8:11 p.m.

"Nothing like announcing our presence by hovering," Donati said.

"No choice," Bruno responded, keeping low as a cascade of bullets chipped away at the planter.

"Those sound like AK-47 rifles," Donati said. "We each have a Beretta with one clip. I'm going to go out on a limb and say that we're outgunned."

Despite bullets slamming into the planter, Bruno and Donais couldn't help but smile at the simultaneous absurdity and correctness of Donati's statement. Suddenly, two gunshots rang out. All three kept low, expecting a stream of bullets to follow. However, when none did, Bruno was the first to poke his head around the edge of the planter. He saw an Italian police officer, wearing the yellow vest of a traffic cop, holding a handgun in his outstretched hands.

The officer didn't notice that behind him was a second subject, the driver who'd earlier grabbed the other end of the filament and who had been running toward the generator to plug it in when his partner went down. Upon hearing the gunshots, the man had turned and dropped the filament, then unslung the assault rifle from his right shoulder. The traffic cop, who was transfixed on the person he'd just dispatched to Allah, had no idea that he was less than a breath away from death when a volley of gunshots brought him back to the present and sent him diving to the ground. Several feet behind him, the second gunman now lay on his back with six dime-sized holes in his chest.

Bruno, Donati, and Donais put their guns back in their shoulder holsters, walked to the bodies, and checked them for any signs of life but found none.

While Donais shut off the generator and Donati cut off the flow of gas from both vehicles, Bruno walked over to the officer. When Bruno returned, Donati asked him what the officer had said.

"He's a traffic cop who was in the right place at the right time, as far as we're concerned. I asked him not to call this in or write his report until he heard from Acardi."

"I guess that name got his attention," Donati said.

"It did. I don't know if Acardi wants what happened here to get out, given the NATO summit. In any event, I'll let him deal with the good officer. Let's take a look at what these two were up to," Bruno said, starting toward the manhole.

The three descended down the ladder. When they reached the bottom, Bruno examined the plastic hoses and fans. "Just as we thought, they were pumping gas into the sewer line."

"And this is probably the igniter," Donati added, looking at the filament that extended into the sewer. "It's a good thing we stopped that guy before he plugged this into the generator."

Bruno needed to tell Acardi what they had found and have him vent out the sewer lines. But when he removed his phone from his pocket, he saw that he had no reception. "I don't have a signal," Bruno said.

Donati and Donais checked their phones and confirmed that they didn't either.

"Let's get to the surface and give Acardi a call."

Once they were out of the manhole, four bars returned to everyone's phone, and Bruno immediately called Acardi, who answered on the second ring. However, they never got beyond a greeting because at that instant there was a massive explosion, and a fireball extending two hundred feet in the air rose in the distance. The line immediately went dead.

"The presidential palace!" Donais exclaimed, looking at the orange and red flames extending into the sky.

The men that Zebari had sent to destroy the NATO Defense College were substantially behind schedule, largely because they hadn't been prepared for the nearly two feet of water that they found in the sewer line. They'd assumed from their past two inspections of the pipe, the last of which had occurred a week ago, that it would be relatively dry. That belief had been further reinforced by a lack of rain in Rome for the past three weeks. What they hadn't counted on was that a large company outside the military zone had hours earlier flushed and cleaned its storage tanks. As a result, the plastic pipes coming from the carrier trucks had to be elevated once they were down in the sewer; here there were no grates in which the men could wedge the pipes to elevate them, as there were in the Quirinal sewer line. Laying the pipes on the water was a nonstarter because the gas would harmlessly disperse into it.

A good ten minutes passed before one of the men came up with a solution, which involved using their shoelaces and shirts to tie the pipes and fans to the steel rungs leading down into the manhole. However, although this solved one problem, it created another: the open end of the plastic pipe was almost right below the uncovered manhole now, and the natural gas was lighter than air, so as they were pumping the gas into the sewer, a significant amount would escape up through the manhole. That problem was partially solved by one of the drivers, who used his pocketknife to remove the covers from his truck's driver and passenger seats and then stretched the material over the manhole opening to create a seal. The team on the other side of the NDC duplicated this procedure.

The routine and layout at the NDC were a terrorist's dream for two reasons. The first was that once a day everyone congregated in one spot—the officers' living quarters, generally referred to as the dorm, which also contained the officers' mess. After 7:00 p.m., everyone was inside the structure since nothing else on the college campus was open.

The second reason was that the sewer line ran directly under the dorm.

At 8:17 p.m. the men saw a red glow that looked to be approximately ten miles away. Knowing that it could only be an explosion and that if they could see it from this distance, it had to be large, they immediately dropped to their knees and gave thanks to Allah for destroying the Quirinal. Figuring that there was no rush, since any police officer in the city who wasn't already at the presidential palace would be there shortly, the men began taking selfies near their LNG carrier trucks, which they would show to their future children and grandchildren as they recounted how they had deprived NATO of not only its current leaders but also those who had been intended to guide it for the next generation.

CHAPTER 14

FOLLOWING THE EXPLOSION, the helicopter that had dropped Bruno, Donati, and Donais on the rooftop patio was recalled, and they were left to their own devices to get back to the Quirinal. After seeing the giant fireball, all expressed doubt that the presidential palace was still intact. The fact that Bruno's call with Acardi, who they knew was at the palace, had gone dead at the time of the explosion reinforced this feeling.

"It looks like the only way we're getting back is by walking," Bruno said, watching the navigation lights from their transport streak into the distance. "It's only five blocks—we can run there in a few minutes."

"Let's do it," Donati said.

Ten minutes later, they encountered the southern security perimeter. The jog had taken longer than anticipated because they'd had to run up a hill, something they hadn't taken into the equation. On top of that, Bruno, a reformed heavy smoker, wasn't in the best shape and had slowed them down.

"I'd forgotten the palace was on a hill," Bruno said, trying to regain his breath.

"Still, not bad for a former smoker," replied Donati, who was breathing hard and also had given up the addiction.

Donais, in contrast, had barely a bead of sweat on her face.

The southern security perimeter consisted of a continuous line of concrete traffic barriers, on top of which were rows of barbed wire extending to a height of six feet. Spaced behind the barriers were numerous six-thousand-watt light plants, each connected to its own generator, that brightly illuminated the area. Military patrols, some in armored vehicles and some on foot, continuously patrolled both sides of the perimeter. There was one entry point, with ten soldiers in front of it. Vehicles that required entry were physically searched and sniffed by a dog trained to detect both explosives and chemicals. Once a vehicle was cleared, the hydraulic bollards across the entry road were lowered to permit passage. Thirty yards beyond the bollards was an armored personnel carrier, with half a dozen troops standing around it.

Bruno approached the entry point and asked one of the guards if he could speak with the officer in charge. Five minutes later, an army major approached. Bruno told him that Deputy Commissioner Dante Acardi had asked Bruno and his colleagues to evaluate the Quirinal's security and explained that they needed to get to the palace as soon as possible. The expression on the officer's face as he looked at the three disheveled investigators indicated that name-dropping wouldn't get anyone inside the barrier, least of all without proper ID. The officer didn't seem to care if Bruno knew Acardi, or even the pope for that matter. His said that his orders were to keep anyone without the proper badge out of the area, and that's what he intended to do.

Bruno backed away from the barrier and rejoined Donati and Donais. "Dropping Acardi's name didn't work. We need authorization to get through the perimeter gate."

"Try Acardi again," Donais said.

"You're right. We just assumed that something happened to him." Bruno tried calling twice, and each time his call was redirected to voice mail. "He's not answering. Let's get off the street and find a bar or restaurant where we can sit down and figure out who can get us past security," Bruno said.

Donati and Donais agreed, and the three began walking toward a restaurant that was fifty yards south of them. They'd gone thirty feet when the officer who'd politely told Bruno to get lost yelled for him to return to the entry gate. When the trio arrived at the barrier, the officer handed his cell phone to Bruno.

"*Pronto*?" Bruno said.

"Thank God you're alive."

Bruno's serious facial expression began to relax. It was Acardi's voice.

"I couldn't believe it when I got your voice mails. I was told that there'd been a shooting a block from the southern perimeter and that two people were killed. Knowing that's where the helicopter took the three of you, I imagined the worst."

"The same here. I thought that you'd been killed when the line between us went dead and I saw the explosion. I tried calling you twice, but I couldn't get through."

"We were disconnected because the cell tower outside the palace was destroyed. Fortunately, there are several others in the area. I was on my cell the two times that you phoned. There's a lot going on."

"The explosion—how bad is the damage?"

"Extensive, with a substantial number of injuries. We're currently trying to control the fires so that they don't spread and make this an even greater calamity. You'll see when you get here. Hand the phone to the major, and I'll give him instructions for where to escort the three of you."

Montanari was sitting at his desk, finishing the last of his cannoli and chasing it down with a Red Bull, when it occurred to him that it had been a while since he'd looked at Conti's server and computer. Since he was now familiar with how to penetrate the company's security protocols, he accessed the server in less than a minute and began looking at any email that had been sent or received since his last intrusion. There were four—two from Zebari and two from Conti.

The four messages were seemingly innocuous and looked like banal business chatter, exhibiting nothing unusual except for bad spelling, odd word spacing, and horrible punctuation, especially the use of exclamation marks in the most unexpected places. The computer genius had a difficult time believing that these mistakes were anything other than intentional since they were common to emails from two different users sharing the same server. That could only mean that the senders were cleverly trying to make the emails appear routine while communicating something entirely different within the text. However, this deception required a decryption key.

Leaning back in his chair, Montanari rubbed his tired, bloodshot eyes. He was reaching to throw away his empty can of Red Bull when the stack of papers piled on the corner of his desk caught his eye. The top page was an email that he'd received from Lisette Donais, someone he knew nothing about other than that she was Bruno and Donati's partner—which was why he had printed her message instead of deleting it, as he normally would with a message from someone he didn't know.

He printed out the four suspicious emails from the server and, following Donais's suggestion, turned the image of the artifact that she'd sent into a template by cutting holes where they would have been on the original. He then placed the first hole over the exclamation mark of Conti's first email. Looking at the underlying text, Montanari had no doubt that he had the decryption key.

Working frantically because of what he was reading, he quickly decrypted the four emails, after which he grabbed his phone and called Bruno. It was 8:20 p.m.

Ragno was dripping with sweat and breathing heavily. He was not only late but extremely late thanks to the veritable sea of adolescents in front of him. Add to that his being fifty pounds overweight, and it was no wonder that he had a pounding headache and felt pressure building in his chest. Ragno took the bottle of aspirin from his pocket and popped two.

The adolescents seemed to be in no hurry and moved with the speed of the US Congress—more interested in talking than in getting to their destination. It was already 2:30 p.m. He could see his destination ahead and assumed, at his current pace, that he was still five minutes away. Loosening his shirt collar and unbuttoning his jacket, he decided to cut that time in half by stepping off the sidewalk and into the street so that he could walk next to the curb, past the students. He figured drivers would rather go around him than explain to a police officer how they had hit a pedestrian, even if he was in the street. Although there were a couple of close calls from drivers who were texting, his strategy worked. He passed the adolescents and figured that in two minutes he'd be at his rendezvous point.

Following Acardi's call with Bruno, Agusta A129 Mangusta attack helicopters from the Italian army raced across Rome toward the NATO Defense College. Acardi's order to the force commander aboard one of the aircraft was concise—confront the LNG drivers and take them into custody if possible, and if that was not possible, make sure they never got a chance to ignite the gas. To a police officer that would have meant asking the men to surrender and, if they refused, calling in a negotiator and then, if that didn't work, a SWAT team. To the military Acardi's order meant something entirely different. It meant telling the drivers to surrender immediately and then, if they refused, punching their ticket to the morgue.

As it so happened, the second scenario occurred. Acardi saw from the three attack helicopters' video feeds that all four terrorists were apparently taking selfies when they heard the Agustas approaching. Before the terrorists could exchange their cell phones for weapons, the force commander pressed his aircraft's external speaker share switch, to relay whatever he said through the speakers of the other attack helicopters. In forceful language, he told the men there was no chance of escape and to surrender. In response, the terrorists grabbed their AK-47 rifles and began shooting at the three aircraft, bouncing several bullets off their armored skin.

Each of the Agusta combat helicopters had a M197 nose-mounted electric cannon on board. Capable of firing up to fifteen hundred rounds per minute, the cannon typically released its 20 mm ammunition in thirty- to fifty-round bursts, each bullet traveling at 3,380 feet per second. Although Hollywood, with its creative script writers, often showed ground combatants holding off their airborne assailants and, in some cases, even blowing them from the sky, in real life the outcome was completely different and predictable. The return gunfire from the three aircraft lasted slightly more than one second, whereupon ninety rounds punched through the four terrorists.

After the terrorists were neutralized, Acardi asked the force commander to clean up the area so that it would appear nothing out of the ordinary had happened. Neither man worried about reporters responding to the sounds of gunfire or circling helicopters since the NDC was in a military zone that was closed to civilian traffic. Residents of the dorm who ventured outside upon hearing the sound of the hovering helicopters and the exchange of gunfire were told by the force commander to go back indoors, an order they immediately complied with.

Acardi informed the commander that his mission was to be considered top secret and was never to be discussed. Additionally, no report was necessary or expected, and the bodies of the terrorists should be disposed of. The lieutenant colonel, a twenty-year veteran, replied that he understood and that the military exercise this evening, using dummies to simulate terrorists, had gone as planned.

CHAPTER 15

I
T WAS 2:32 p.m., seventeen minutes past the time Conti
had told Giancarlo Ragno to phone his contact, when
Ragno reached his rendezvous point. Conti hadn't been all
that specific about the location for the meet, saying only that
he was to go to the Fifteenth Street NW side of the White
House. Now that Ragno was here, he saw that security was
extremely tight, with armed guards spaced every twenty feet
between the White House fence and the concrete barrier ten
feet in front of it. Each guard was carrying an assault rifle and
scanning the crowd.

The fact that he was the only person he could see who was
carrying a suitcase didn't cause Ragno a great deal of concern.
In Washington, just as in any tourist-oriented city, people
were always checking out of hotels and taking their luggage
with them so that they could see one last site before going
to the airport. However, that perspective wasn't necessarily
shared by the guards thirty feet in front of him. He noticed
that they were focusing on the suitcase he was pulling and
speaking into their mics. No one was moving toward him yet,
but they were giving him a look that said they intended to do
just that. That might have caused him a great deal of concern
had it not been for the diplomatic tags on the bag and his

133

diplomatic passport. With an expression that said "you can't touch me," he looked one of the guards directly in the eye as he put his beefy hand into his pocket and withdrew the phone that Conti had given him.

Jonathan Kincaid had enlisted in the marine corps at age eighteen. A year after he entered, he had successfully applied for scout sniper training school. He had then served six additional years in the corps before deciding to get out because his parents were in failing health, and being an only child, he needed to watch over of them. Since they lived in northern Virginia, he had looked for a government job in DC—something where he could protect the public. The Secret Service, FBI, DEA, and a few other alphabet companies were options. He had eventually decided to apply to the Secret Service, and after excelling at marksmanship, he had become a countersniper.

Today he was stationed on top of the White House, looking at Fifteenth Street NW for a man whose physical description he'd been given. The person he was looking for was expected to be carrying or rolling a suitcase and was scheduled to make a phone call at 2:15 p.m. while standing outside the White House fence, something Kincaid and every other agent had been ordered to prevent at any cost. Therefore, if he saw a person matching the suspect's description on Fifteenth Street NW with a suitcase and a phone in his hand, Kincaid was to kill him without hesitation. The bureaucracy would handle the fallout. The reason the agents had been given was that the suitcase contained a dirty bomb and the phone was the trigger. Kincaid didn't think he needed any more reason than that.

It was 2:32 p.m. when Kincaid saw the man. When he did, he announced the location over his service mic and saw the agents along the perimeter fence turn their heads toward him. There was no sign of a phone in the man's hands, which was one of two reasons the agents on the fence didn't immediately kill him. The other was that his suitcase had a diplomatic sticker affixed to it, something that hadn't been mentioned in their BOLO alert. No one wanted to kill an innocent. Therefore, the agent at whom the suspect was staring was calling his supervisor for clarification when the man reached into his pocket.

In the current environment, when a local law enforcement or federal officer killed someone, the media immediately wanted the officer's scalp unless there was a notarized affidavit from the deceased saying it was all right for the officer to take the person's life. Even then, the family was likely to sue the officer for violating the decedent's civil right to be a murderer and an asshole. Therefore, Kincaid realized that killing anyone in front of the White House would land him in jail, despite the director's statement that the bureaucracy would handle it. In politispeak that meant that the shooter would take the fall, and the bureaucracy would get off the hook because politicians were exceptionally good at one thing—placing the blame on others and covering their asses. Nevertheless, knowing he had no more than a second or two to react, Kincaid made his decision and took the shot. He'd be either a hero or an inmate by the end of the day.

The officer in charge of the southern perimeter escorted Bruno, Donati, and Donais past the Quirinal's interior security, which was one hundred yards below the top of the hill, before he excused himself and said that he must return to his post. The three investigators continued up the stone path toward the summit, which was not yet in their view, and nothing could have prepared them for what they saw when they reached the top—the presidential palace was completely intact.

"Surprised?" Acardi asked, startling the three investigators, who hadn't seen him approach.

"I don't understand why the Quirinal wasn't destroyed. We heard the explosion and the fireball seemed to be over this hill," Donais said.

"The explosion that you saw didn't happen on the palace grounds, it occurred directly north of it. Looking at the presidential palace from the south, which is where you were standing, you would have no depth perception because the Quirinal sits in the center of a hill. Therefore, it seemed as if the fireball came from here."

"And what about Washington, DC, and the NATO Defense College?" Bruno asked, recalling what Montanari had told him.

"Stopped, thanks to the quick investigative work performed by the three of you and Mr. Montanari. Let me explain."

The three investigators moved closer to Acardi, not wanting to miss a word.

"Here's my take on what happened. The terrorists' plan, judging from the photos texted to me a short time ago from the manhole near the southern perimeter, was to pump gas into both ends of the sewer line that runs beneath the Quirinal and ignite it. I suppose they believed that the explosion would cause a conflagration and kill everyone at the NATO summit dinner—a good assumption if the four truckloads of LNG had filled the entire sewer line and been ignited."

"Then why didn't everything go up in flames?" Donati asked.

"You can ask the natural gas expert when he arrives. However, thinking about this logically, I don't believe that the gas had enough time to disperse through the entire line. Otherwise, the entire sewer line would have exploded and not just the section north of the palace. Whatever the reason, we came within a hair of losing four heads of state and the entire NATO hierarchy."

"You said that both the NDC and the White House attacks were stopped?" Donais said.

"The army neutralized the threat at the NDC, and the American Secret Service killed the minister of justice outside the White House fence and recovered the dirty bomb."

"Deaths from the gas explosion?" Donais asked.

"None. But fifty-two civilians were injured, all of whom were working or living in the buildings lining the street under which the northern sewer line ran. However, my report will list four dead—the drivers involved in pumping gas from their carrier trucks into underground storage tanks near the Quirinal. Since the incident at the NDC never occurred, there were no casualties. Unofficially, the four men involved in the attack were killed and taken care of."

Bruno understood that the bodies of those four terrorists would never be found, and the expressions on his colleagues' faces indicated that they recognized this too.

"What do we do about Conti?" Bruno asked. "He's responsible not only for what happened here but also for the dirty bomb."

"What would you do?" Acardi asked.

"Since none of the evidence we have can be used against him in a court of law, because it was obtained illegally, the only way to stop Conti is to kill him."

"I'm not opposed to that option," Acardi replied. "However, we should take it as fact that from this point forward, he'll probably never leave his rig. Therefore, he will be almost impossible to get at, and his company will continue to generate huge profits, which I'm sure will fund future acts of aggression."

"I think that's something that we all agree on," Donati replied.

"What about the terrorists whose identities we gleaned from Conti's computer?" Donais asked. "Is the AISI acting on that?"

"Yes and no. Yes, in that they are now persons of interest in the terrorist database. No, in that some are Italian citizens with jobs who have committed no known crimes. And even though they took shortcuts to citizenship—with no evidence of bribes or other illegality on their part, it's Ragno's crime and not theirs."

"Our goal is to cut off the head of the snake before it gets a chance to strike again," Bruno interjected. "I may have a suggestion on how to make that happen."

"Which is?" Acardi asked.

Bruno proceeded to tell him.

"That's a very innovative plan, and I'm in. All I ask in return is that you give me a job when I get out of prison."

CHAPTER 16

THE NEWS ANCHOR indicated that what earlier had been thought to be one explosion just north of the presidential palace had in fact been three. The first had occurred when a bolt of lightning struck one of two gas tanker trucks fueling a large subterranean storage tank. That ignited the second tanker and then, in a third explosion, the fuel within the subterranean tank. The last explosion had taken out the adjacent sewer line, imploding it and creating a huge canyon in the earth that damaged or destroyed thirty nearby buildings. Four people had been killed and fifty-two injured in the explosions. The anchor went on to say that President Orsini had promised a full and transparent investigation of the incident.

Conti turned off the television and slumped in his chair.

"There's no news report of an explosion in Washington," Rotolo said. "Years of planning wasted."

"We just have to succeed once, while our enemies have to be successful in stopping us one hundred percent of the time. No one can maintain that percentage. Sooner or later, we'll seriously hurt our enemies. Patience."

"Why did the government lie about what happened?"

"They're not about to tell the good citizens of Italy that four heads of state and the brain trust of NATO came within a hair of being killed. That would undermine everyone's confidence in the government. Neither will the United States reveal that they stopped the explosion of a dirty bomb yards from the White House—however that happened."

"The good news is that those who could implicate us are dead."

"Most of them," Conti corrected. "All except for our helicopter pilot and the three troublesome investigators who somehow managed to stay alive. It's time we clean house."

After discussing what they needed to, Conti began working on his computer. Rotolo, meanwhile, went to his room, retrieved a small black bag, and took it to the helicopter, whose pilot was getting a bite to eat in the kitchen. Conti downloaded his computer data onto a flash drive and then double-clicked on BleachBit, a software program made famous by Hillary Clinton. This would shred files, prevent recovery of data, and wipe clean the disks on both his computer and his server, to destroy any trace of what had been deleted.

When Rotolo returned, Conti handed him both the computer and the flash drive. "Have the pilot throw these into the sea, and make sure you tell him that he must be exactly five miles east of this rig when he does so. I erased everything on them because I'm naturally paranoid and can't take a chance that even a small fragment of data could survive."

Rotolo took both devices and went to get the pilot. Ten minutes later, the Airbus AS365 Dauphin helicopter lifted off the helipad, turned east, and headed out to sea. As it did, Rotolo watched from the top of the derrick, using the GPS tracker in his hands to follow the aircraft's progress until it finally came to a hover exactly five miles from the platform, whereupon he typed a phone number into his cell phone and pressed send. Less than a second later, a brief fireball, caused by the detonation of a brick of C-4 plastic explosive hidden under the pilot's seat, appeared in the sky. The wreckage plunged a thousand feet straight down into the water, floated briefly, then sank to the seabed. Rotolo would later report to the authorities in Monopoli that his company's corporate helicopter was long overdue and was presumed to have crashed while in transit from the oil platform to the mainland. Since the ensuing search would be conducted in that seven-mile stretch west of the platform, neither the remains of the pilot nor the helicopter would ever be found. In a body of water as large as the Adriatic Sea, it would be easier to find a needle in a haystack.

Sargon Zebari was watching the BBC reporter recount ad nauseam the government's explanation of the explosions outside the Quirinal. The circle of data repeated so often that he switched to other news services in the hope that he might hear something about the attack on the NDC. However, after an hour of again listening to the same banter, he had to assume that both attacks had failed. His only hope of salvaging something from his years of work was that the attack on Washington would ultimately prove successful. That belief was crushed two hours later when, listening to Sky News, he learned that Italy's minister of justice had suffered a fatal heart attack in Washington, DC. There was no mention of a suitcase with a diplomatic sticker on it.

Zebari angrily slammed his fist into the cheaply constructed wall beside him, putting a large hole in it. He realized that the blowback for the dirty bomb attempt would be significant. US intelligence agencies weren't the inept organizations that they were sometimes portrayed to be in media and movies. They were highly disciplined and well-funded agencies that eventually ferreted out the truth and shared that information with the military. There were very few countries where America couldn't put a Hellfire missile into his residence or vehicle. Iran was one of those, which meant he wasn't returning to Iraq anytime soon—if ever.

President Enrico Orsini, Dante Acardi, and the three partners of BD&D Investigations sat at a highly polished rectangular conference table within the president's office. It had been two days since the attacks, and the looks on their faces were still anything but joyful because they couldn't legally arrest the persons who they knew were responsible for these terrorist acts.

"If I understand correctly," Orsini said, looking at Bruno, "your computer expert, Mr. Montanari, who's had a very colorful past from what my staff has told me, can't rehack Conti's server and computer because he believes they've both been destroyed."

"That's correct."

"We all know that the files and messages that Mr. Montanari illegally obtained can't be admitted into any court of law. With the computer and server gone, we need another source of incriminating evidence to convict him and his accomplices."

"Can we obtain a court order to search his rig and possibly his house in Caprarola?" Donati asked. "Maybe we'll find something there."

"On what basis would we ask for a warrant?" asked the president. "Curiosity? Understand that I'm eternally grateful that you prevented the terrorists from igniting the gas at the southern perimeter and gave us information that stopped their attack on the NDC and the White House. However, don't expect to get a court order to search Conti's office or residences without specifying what we're looking for and why we believe it's there. His orphan-to-billionaire story has made him a national hero. If we accuse him without proof, I'll be out of office, and the four of you will be security guards at a sports venue."

"Stating the obvious, a snake doesn't change its nature," Acardi said. "Conti will eventually succeed with an attack that will have profound consequences for the West and probably Italy. He's well-funded, thanks to the enormous revenue his oil platforms generate."

"Which is why we're here—to discuss how to legally take him and anyone associated with him down."

"By the way," Donati said, "I was told by the deputy commissioner here that our minister of justice was shot by an American Secret Service sniper outside the White House fence. How did the Americans cover that up and turn his death into a heart attack?"

"Luck, mostly." Orsini went on to explain what he'd been told by President Ballinger. Upon receiving the warning from Italy, White House security had begun looking for Ragno. Several agents were already moving toward him as he was taking the phone from his pocket. Therefore, once he was killed by the sniper, the crowd couldn't get close because Secret Service agents were already around the body. One of them put his jacket over him and covered the bullet hole.

"Will there be an autopsy?" Bruno asked.

"It's already been done. I'm told by President Ballinger that the official autopsy will document that a myocardial infarction caused the minister's death. I asked that he be cremated and sent back home in an urn."

"Do we know how Ragno got the suitcase to Washington?"

"The minister of foreign affairs gave him a diplomatic passport and sticker for the suitcase carrying the radioactive material. The process of how that happened is something that I'm going to look into before I fire him for being either complicit in what occurred or an idiot."

"Does President Ballinger know about the emails and the artifact?" Bruno asked.

"I didn't have a chance to discuss those matters with him earlier, but I will when we speak in a few minutes."

"What do you expect he'll do when he learns the entire story?" Bruno asked.

"What do I expect the leader of the most powerful military on the planet to do after he learns who's responsible for an attempt on his life? That doesn't take much of an imagination. Better order more urns." With that Orsini excused himself.

At the request of the Italian head of state, the call between President Orsini and President Ballinger wasn't recorded. Since both presidential offices automatically recorded all incoming and outgoing calls, which were later transcribed for the historical record, both men went to their respective residential offices for their conversation. Since the president of Italy spoke passable English, no interpreter was necessary.

Orsini began by giving President Ballinger a detailed update regarding the attack on the Quirinal and the attempted destruction of the NDC before segueing into the emails linking both Antonio Conti and Sargon Zebari to these attacks and the dirty bomb brought to Washington. He didn't mention how the information had been obtained, and Ballinger didn't ask.

"I'd like us to work together to bring these terrorists to justice without burdening our court system," Orsini said. His voice told the leader of the free world that he was deadly serious.

Ballinger, seemingly surprised at what he'd just heard, momentarily paused before responding. "I agree. However, that would necessitate that the United States take the lead and that we receive unquestioning support from you."

"That's to be expected. However, the result must be opaque, meaning that everything that occurs either will be attributed to an accident or will have never happened."

The conversation continued in this vein for another three minutes. President Ballinger then said that he'd phone Orsini back when he could provide the details for a plan of action.

Orsini walked back to his office. The eyes of the three investigators and the deputy commissioner of the Polizia di Stato followed him as he retook his seat at the head of the conference table.

"I just spoke to President Ballinger, and he's agreed to help us."

"How?" Acardi asked.

"He didn't mention how. But I can tell you from the tenor of the conversation that Conti, Zebari, and anyone else involved in these attacks are soon going to have an extremely bad day."

CHAPTER 17

FOLLOWING HIS CALL with the president of Italy, Ballinger pressed a speed-dial number on his desktop phone and was immediately connected with Chinese president Fai Liu. Ballinger relayed to President Liu the substance of his conversation with Orsini and his desire to take action against Conti, Zebari, and their followers. Liu quickly voiced his agreement, providing the necessary second vote for the use of Nemesis. After ending his call with the president of China, Ballinger pressed a second speed-dial number, this one for Lieutenant Colonel Doug Cray, and summoned Cray to the residence.

Cray's philosophy for dealing with extremists was simplistic—kill them before they could harm innocents, sending them to whatever God they believed in, preferably in pieces, so that assembly would be required. The lieutenant colonel was six feet tall with sandy brown hair and piercing blue eyes. He had a jogger's physique and looked like a college professor rather than the commander of Nemesis, an off-the-books organization named after the Greek goddess of retribution that had been formed by President Ballinger and President Liu of China to aggressively act against those who would do either nation harm.

Nemesis's cover within the US government was the White House Statistical Analysis Division, an office that reported solely to the president. It was located at the Raven Rock Mountain Complex in Maryland, also known as Site R, which was the military's backup to the Pentagon. The remoteness and high security at the site allowed those within the organization to operate outside the scrutiny of bureaucratic Washington.

There were ten members of Nemesis—two analysts, three support staff, and five operatives—and its existence was known to only thirteen people. The seed for the formation of the organization had been the recent kidnappings of both President Ballinger and President Liu and the fact that both Washington and Beijing's militaries and intelligence agencies had failed to find and rescue them. Instead, their lives had been saved by a rogue group of individuals operating independently from their bureaucratic organizations. This had led Presidents Ballinger and Liu to use these individuals to start Nemesis, an organization that was answerable only to the two heads of state. The group's first mission, preventing a whack job from detonating nuclear weapons within Beijing and Shanghai, had concluded just two months ago. Its second mission was about to be assigned.

When Cray arrived at the White House, he was immediately taken to the residence by his Secret Service escort. He was greeted by the president in the Solarium, which was located on the third floor and had a panoramic view of Washington. The president wasn't someone to beat around the bush. He directed the lieutenant colonel to one of the two club chairs facing the window and began speaking before Cray's butt hit the seat. President Ballinger laid out Nemesis's next mission, which was to eliminate Antonio

Conti and Sargon Zebari and anyone the group could identify who was working with him, in such a way that there would be no blowback to either the United States or China. The how of this would be left up to Cray, but he had only three hours to come up with a plan because in exactly 180 minutes, he and his team would be wheels up in a C-17 transport aircraft that was scheduled to depart from Joint Base Andrews.

Within Nemesis, Lieutenant Colonel Doug Cray was the *capo di tutti capi*, meaning he was at the top of the food chain, and Matt Moretti was his lead field operative. Comparatively speaking, their operational skills were similar to those of M and James Bond in an Ian Fleming novel. Moretti stood six feet, three inches tall, had a chiseled face and hazel eyes, and weighed 230 pounds. He was in his midthirties, and gray had yet to intrude into his close-cut black hair. An ex–Army Ranger with a chest full of medals, including the Distinguished Service Cross and Silver Star, the second- and third-highest awards from a grateful nation, he had been on the fast track for major when he and Cray were in a helicopter crash in Afghanistan. Moretti and Cray were the only survivors, and although Cray was largely unharmed, Moretti was a physical wreck. Therefore, after spending one year in rehab, and with his ongoing physical issues possibly unresolvable, he had been given a pat on the back and a medical discharge. Unable to find anything that gave him the satisfaction of being a Ranger, he had descended into alcoholism.

It was Cray who had eventually talked his friend out of the gutter and gotten him a civilian job as an archivist with the government, a position Moretti hated but took to begin his rehabilitation away from the bottle and his self-pity. In time Moretti got his head screwed on straight and his back straightened out, and he was the first person that Cray had selected for Nemesis.

"Ten minutes to taxi," the crew chief yelled to Moretti, who was standing behind the tail ramp of the C-17 Globemaster III transport aircraft with his cell phone pressed hard against his left ear, copying down the information that President Ballinger had given Cray. Two of the C-17's four engines were already started, and the pilot was turning over the third, significantly increasing the decibel level and making it even more difficult to hear. Moretti finished his call and stuffed the small piece of paper on which he'd recorded Cray's information into his pants pocket. As he was doing this, the number four engine came to life, and he dug the earplugs that the crew chief had given him out of his other pocket and placed them in his ears.

As Moretti was looking down the tarmac, he saw a black Chevy Suburban with heavily tinted windows and a Maryland license plate racing toward the aircraft. The vehicle parked alongside the tail ramp, and the driver and passenger, both wearing dark suits, conservative ties, and sunglasses, got out and unloaded two wheeled carrier cases from the cargo compartment. Both cases contained equipment that Cray had requested from the president after building a plan of action with Moretti. Once the cases were signed for, the crew chief secured both on the aircraft.

Starting up the loading ramp, Moretti waved Yan He, Jack Bonaquist, and Han Li, the other three operatives in Nemesis, to follow him on board. Five minutes later, the giant aircraft lifted its tail ramp and started to taxi. Given takeoff priority by the tower, the 174-foot-long, 55-foot-tall aircraft, with a wingspan of nearly 170 feet, turned right onto runway 19, aligned its nose wheel on the centerline, and accelerated smoothly. A little more than halfway down the 11,318-foot-long, 200-foot-wide concrete runway, it lifted off and slowly turned north.

When the Nemesis team stepped off the C-17 at the Ciampino airport near Rome, Moretti and Yan He were the first to walk down the tail ramp, pulling the two wheeled crates off the aircraft along with their gear. Han Li and Jack Bonaquist followed, hauling their gear and two bags of weapons and ammunition that would have been the envy of the NRA. Up until two months ago, there'd been a fifth member of the team, Major Peter Cancelliere. His death in China, while preventing terrorists from setting off nuclear weapons in both Beijing and Shanghai, still weighed heavily on the minds of each member of the team. Cancelliere's replacement, twenty-six-year-old staff sergeant Blaine McGough from the marines' Force Recon, had been selected only yesterday by Cray, who'd looked into the background of hundreds of current and former military personnel before making his decision.

Presently, the newest member of the team was trying to get out of an Afghan village alive after kidnapping a Taliban leader. If he could make it to the rendezvous point, a helo would transport both him and the terrorist asshole he'd captured to Camp Dwyer, where a CIA officer was waiting to take his captive to God-knows-where for interrogation. Although McGough didn't know about his pending transfer to Nemesis, it wouldn't have made any difference if he had, because his only concern at the moment was dodging increasingly heavy weapons fire on his way to the helo.

With the NATO conference still going on in Rome, the arrival of the C-17 at Ciampino didn't seem out of the ordinary to anyone at the airport who watched it land. The Globemaster parked in a recessed area next to an ICH-47F Chinook helicopter, and the four operatives deplaned and hauled their gear and the equipment cases from one aircraft to the other. Moments later, the pilot spun up the Chinook's rotors and gently lifted off the tarmac, putting the aircraft on a southeasterly heading and accelerating to 195 miles per hour. It took one hour and thirty minutes to reach the barren field just outside Monopoli where a black Mercedes SUV was waiting for them, with keys on the driver's seat.

The team's rally point, which was military jargon for a location to reorganize, was loaded in the vehicle's navigation system. Moretti was the driver, and he followed the route that was set for him. Thirteen minutes later, as directed by the navigation system's feminine voice, he turned off the main highway and onto a gravel road, which twisted and turned beside a coastal rock formation that rose twenty feet above the roadway and partitioned them from the Adriatic Sea. Eventually, the road ended at a deserted cove.

As Matt Moretti, Han Li, Jack Bonaquist, and Yan He exited the vehicle, they saw an inflatable boat with a very large engine in the rear resting on the sand, tied to one of the shoreline boulders. The F740 Combat Rubber Raiding Craft, referred to among special forces as a CRRC, was fifteen feet, five inches by six feet, three inches and weighed 320 pounds. Surprisingly nimble in the water, it was powered by a fifty-five-horsepower engine that pushed it along at over twenty-one miles per hour.

Yan He, a lieutenant colonel in the People's Liberation Army, grabbed his gear bag and one of the equipment cases from the rear of the vehicle and headed for the inflatable. He was thirty-six years old, one month older than Moretti, and had the wide shoulders and narrow waist of a swimmer. Standing six feet, two inches tall, with close-cropped black hair and black eyes, he had both the posture and the focused demeanor of a career military officer.

Right behind him was Han Li, who unloaded her gear bag along with the second equipment case. No one would suspect that the stunningly beautiful and athletic, five-foot-eleven woman, with porcelain-like skin, long brunette hair, and black opal–colored eyes, had been China's premier assassin prior to joining Nemesis. Nor would they know that the other operatives considered her the deadliest member of Nemesis.

Moretti and Bonaquist removed the last of the bags from the vehicle and proceeded to the inflatable. Jack Bonaquist, a former Secret Service officer who previously had spent eight years with the FBI's Hostage Rescue Team, was the tallest member of the team at six feet eight inches. With jet-black hair, blue eyes, and a square-jawed face that reflected the sternness of someone who did not mince words, he was the most intimidating operative.

"Let's get suited up," Moretti said. "It'll be dark in a few minutes."

Everyone silently retrieved their wetsuits from their gear bags, along with their specially engineered headsets, and changed. While Moretti and Han Li placed the equipment cases in the inflatable, Yan He and Bonaquist took four 9 mm MP5 submachine guns and spare magazines from the weapons bags and put them in the craft. They then dragged the CRRC into the water and pulled themselves in.

Even though Conti's oil platform was only seven miles away, it took thirty minutes in the heavy seas to reach it. By that time, it was pitch-black except for a ten-foot radius around the platform, which was illuminated by perimeter lights that exposed the dock area and would expose the CRRC when it drew closer.

"I don't see anyone near the dock," Bonaquist said, speaking into his headset mic as he wiped the ocean spray from his eyes.

Moretti, doing his best to hold the CRRC in position in the turbulent sea just outside the perimeter lighting, nodded in agreement, although with the undulation of the craft, no one saw his response.

"The unknown is their surveillance system," Bonaquist added, "although my guess is that Conti doesn't have one because he doesn't want to record arrivals and departures from his rig."

A wave hit Moretti square in the face, and he spit out a mouthful of water. "Irrespective of the fact that we have President Ballinger, President Liu, and President Orsini expecting us to resolve a situation that can't be rectified in any other manner," he said, "we can't loiter here forever. We're going in."

Moretti steered the CRRC into the perimeter lighting and pulled abeam of the dock, after which Yan He and Bonaquist jumped onto the steel grate decking and tied the craft to the two cleats beside it. Once the CRRC was secure, they each grabbed a rifle and stood guard. Moretti and Han Li removed the equipment from their cases. They then secured it with plastic ties to the decking behind a pillar, making them almost impossible to spot. Moretti then powered up the devices and verified that each was working by pressing the self-check button on each. He received a green light on both devices.

"I don't think Conti or Rotolo is going to like what's coming," Moretti told Han Li. "Let's get back to shore so that we can set things up and ruin his day a little more." With that, all four returned to the craft. Once everyone was on board, they untied from the cleats and left the platform.

One of the devices left on the platform was an electromagnetic personnel interdiction control, or EPIC weapon, which emitted a silent electromagnetic pulse, or EMP, that penetrated walls as easily as a knife cut through butter. Temporarily scrambling the nerve endings in a person's inner ear and causing severe nausea, it also affected one's sense of balance—which was why the four operatives wore specially engineered headsets. The other piece of electronic equipment left on the platform was an interface box that routed every telecommunications signal to and from Conti's cell tower first to a US government satellite and then to the highly modified phone in Moretti's gear bag.

Blowing up the rig would have been the simplest option but, in the brief time that Cray and Moretti had to formulate a plan between the meeting with President Ballinger and the aircraft's departure, they concluded that the pristine Italian coastline, along with the area's fish and wildlife, would be adversely affected for decades by the oil spill that would follow. Therefore, they considered plan B, which was to board the rig, put two into the heads of Conti and Rotolo, and throw their bodies overboard. However, on reflection, they had rejected this option too because it eliminated the possibility of extracting valuable intel from Conti and Rotolo, something they believed would save lives and lead to the capture or killing of others involved in Conti's terror network.

When they were seemingly at a dead end, it was Cray, who had formerly worked at the US Army Intelligence and Security Command, also known as INSCOM, which was functionally part of the NSA, who had come up with plan C.

Twenty-seven minutes after leaving the oil platform, the team stepped onshore and changed out of their wetsuits. Putting their gear into the back of the SUV, they drove back to the helicopter and waited for the call they knew would come.

The emergency number that Conti called to request a medevac didn't connect him to the hospital in Monopoli but rather, thanks to the communications interface box, redirected him to the phone that Moretti was holding. The ex–Army Ranger's mother was Italian, and Moretti still spoke the language passably, although Conti was so sick that he wouldn't have noticed any nuance in dialect or regional pronunciation.

So far, Cray and Moretti's plan was going according to script, although their military experience had taught them that things rarely stayed that way. Rummaging through one of the plastic containers aboard the Chinook medevac helicopter that had transported them from Rome, Moretti and Bonaquist donned medical scrubs and draped stethoscopes around their necks as the pilot lifted off and headed toward the Conti Petroleum platform. Five minutes later, they stepped onto the rig's helipad, each wearing headphones to protect them from the EMP pulse and surgical masks and headcovers so that neither Rotolo nor Conti would recognize Moretti. They were greeted by a wobbly-legged Rotolo, who'd apparently been told of their imminent arrival. He led them to Conti's room, stopping once on the way to dry-heave.

"Take him to the aircraft and strap him in," Moretti said outside the door marked 01. "I've got this."

The expression on Rotolo's face was one of relief. He was clearly eager to get to the medevac and make it one step closer to a hospital. Bonaquist, who had received a fair amount of life support training in his former life as a Secret Service agent, led Rotolo to the helicopter and started a dextrose IV drip that included a sedative, putting Conti's number two into a deep sleep within seconds. He then strapped Rotolo's arms and legs to the cot.

Entering Conti's room, Moretti found his patient lying on his back, his face white as a sheet. The former Army Ranger sat on the bed beside Conti and did a few doctorly things, such as putting a stethoscope to Conti's chest, which he did quickly because the EMP made him feel nauseous the second he removed his headset. Afterward, Moretti shook his head in concern, as scripted, and told Conti that he and Rotolo were headed to the hospital. As he was saying this, Conti looked at him curiously. The man seemed to have noticed that Moretti had removed his headphones and then put them back on. However, he was apparently so nauseous that his curiosity passed quickly. Just like Rotolo, he wanted to get to the hospital quickly, and asking questions would only slow that departure.

Once Moretti and Conti were in the helicopter, Bonaquist started Conti's IV, putting him quickly to sleep. He and Moretti then went to the docking platform, retrieved the EPIC device and communications interface box, turned them off, and brought them on board the helicopter. None of the oil workers saw this because they were all sick in their cabins. That would change in a few minutes with the cessation of the EMP pulse. But by that time, the Nemesis operatives would be long gone.

After liftoff, the medevac turned east, away from Monopoli, and headed into the Adriatic Sea to the coordinates that President Liu had given President Ballinger and that

Moretti had received from Cray and written down prior to departing for Rome.

Twenty miles off the shore of Monopoli and thirteen miles from the Conti Petroleum rig, at the coordinates provided by President Liu, Bonaquist spotted a submarine periscope. As the medevac went into a hover, a cigar-shaped Chinese submarine broke the surface of the water, and the Chinook descended toward it.

CHAPTER 18

THE CHANGZHENG 6 was an SSBN Xia-class submarine, meaning it was nuclear-powered and capable of launching missiles. Its normal patrol area wasn't anywhere near Italy, an area that China considered far removed from where it needed to protect its shipping lanes and confront its geopolitical and economic enemies. Therefore, when the captain of the Changzheng 6 received an eyes-only message from President Liu ordering him to these coordinates to pick up two prisoners, with instructions on where they were to be taken, he knew the prisoners were enemies of the state whose destination needed to be kept secret.

The submarine had been circling the rendezvous area for some time when the captain saw the approaching medevac through his periscope. After ordering the sub to surface, he went on deck with several crew members to receive his human cargo and supervise their transport to quarters under heavy guard. Twenty minutes after the Changzheng 6 surfaced, it closed its hatch and began pumping seawater into the bottom of its ballast tanks. This replaced the air within and allowed the submarine to descend to its cruise depth of four hundred feet, where it would remain for the rest of its journey.

With Conti and Rotolo out of the way, President Ballinger called to thank Orsini for his cooperation. He also extended his appreciation to Bruno, Donati, Donais, and Acardi, who'd been summoned to Orsini's office for the call.

After the circular back-patting session was complete, and as POTUS was ending the call with a bevy of flattering remarks, Bruno interjected. "Mr. President, I think you should know that our success in stopping these attacks was due in large part to the efforts of a computer expert, Indro Montanari." He then went on to explain how the semi-reformed hacker had learned and shared the details of the attacks by hacking into the server shared by Conti and Zebari.

"Get him on the line," Ballinger said. "I want to speak to this unsung hero."

Montanari answered the call with a mouth full of cannoli. Once he learned that Orsini and Ballinger were on the phone, he tried to swallow quickly and began choking. After taking a swig of Red Bull to wash everything down and clear his throat, he accepted both presidents' thanks for what he'd done.

"Given your undeniable expertise at hacking into computer systems, perhaps you can help us find the whereabouts of Sargon Zebari," Ballinger said, apparently realizing that he was speaking to a valuable resource in his fight against the terrorist leader.

"I may already know," Montanari responded. "I installed a program in Conti's server the first time I hacked into it, which, before the server went dark, gave me the geographic coordinates of the two computers that sent and received emails through the server."

"Then you know where Zebari is hiding?" Ballinger asked.

"I believe you'll find him in Rasht, Iran. Want the address?"

Neither Ballinger nor anyone else said a word for ten seconds, after which they requested and received the information from Montanari.

After the call ended, President Ballinger summoned Cray to the executive residence. Thirty minutes later, the lieutenant colonel entered the Solarium.

"I can't order the military or an alphabet agency to go after him," Ballinger explained during their discussion. "If our people were caught or killed, it would give the Iranians a huge propaganda platform on the world stage and could even lead to an armed conflict. Moreover, Washington is like a sieve. There are no secrets here because knowledge is power. No bureaucrat ever increased their political or monetary standing by keeping something to themselves. Therefore, it's again up to Nemesis to protect our country and punch the ticket for this piece of shit."

"At a minimum I'll need aerial surveillance to locate, track, and target him," said Cray. "Also, because he's in Iran, I'll need a stealth drone to penetrate Iranian airspace without being detected."

The president sat back in his desk chair and took a deep breath as if contemplating what he was about to say. "We always knew that Nemesis would need additional capabilities and that these would be dictated by the requirements of our missions. Therefore, it's time to acquire a drone. Any suggestions?"

"The Lockheed Martin MQ-170 Sentinel. It has the radar signature of a hummingbird and is the only drone that could slip in and out of Iran and take out a target without being detected. We'll also need a UAV pilot for this aircraft and his crew chief."

"This is the drone that looks like a mini B-2 stealth bomber?"

"Yes, sir. It's visually identical to the RQ-170 reconnaissance version, except this variant has weapons in its internal bay. It still has some visual and electronic surveillance capabilities, but not nearly as robust as the surveillance version."

"Then that's what you'll get."

"Sir, that may not be possible. This multiuse version was introduced only six months ago, and production is still gearing up. Currently, the DOD and CIA are the sole users of this type of Sentinel, and each has received only two to date, even though they've placed orders for substantially more. It's safe to say that neither will give one up without a fight. It'll be messy. They'll question why POTUS needs a stealth drone, especially this highly classified weapons variant."

"Horse trading is the soul of Washington negotiations. Let me see what I can do."

While Cray looked on, President Ballinger used the phone in the Solarium to call Secretary of Defense Jim Rosen. Putting the call on speaker, Ballinger told the secretary that one of his MQ-170 Sentinels, along with a senior UAV pilot and his crew chief, were to be transferred immediately to the White House's Statistical Analysis Division.

"Mr. President, I can't carry out my assigned missions if you take away the most sophisticated drone in my fleet. Can I ask why your analysts need a weapons-capable stealth drone? Wouldn't the reconnaissance version be better suited to whatever it is you want to surveil?"

"I need this model's radar-evading capabilities to go where I'm not invited and defend American assets if needed."

The slight hesitation and stutter in Rosen's voice indicated that he didn't believe any of what he was being told, but he wasn't about to call his boss a liar. "Mr. President, the next two multiuse Sentinels produced by Lockheed Martin will be going to the CIA. The DOD won't receive its next MQ-170 until six months after that delivery."

"I realize it's a sacrifice, Jim, so that's why I'm ordering that the DOD take delivery of both CIA drones in addition to keeping the one you're expecting. I also appreciate your discretion in this matter, as this presidential capability is on a strict need-to-know basis. Therefore, compartmentalize everything on this transfer, including the personnel."

In Washington no one fully believed anything they were told. Anyone who worked with bureaucrats, military or civilian, understood that lies, platitudes, and placebos all melded into one. However, they did believe in quid pro quo. The deal that Ballinger proposed would give two extra Sentinels to the DOD. The fact that they would be taken from the CIA made this transaction particularly sweet.

That afternoon, Adam Daller, a US Air Force captain assigned to Creech Air Force Base in Nevada, and his crew chief, Master Sergeant Peter Sherman, received their transfer orders to the White House Statistical Analysis Division and thereby became the eleventh and twelfth members of Nemesis.

Cray left Joint Base Andrews in the backseat of the air force fighter and landed two and a half hours later at Creech. Rosen, who'd arranged the transportation, also had ordered Captain Adam Daller to be waiting in the operations center conference room when Cray arrived.

Daller was five feet, eleven inches tall and twenty-four years old and had closely cropped black hair. He was tan, had six-pack abs, and had a face that bore a faint resemblance to the singer-actor Nick Jonas, which meant that he garnered more than his fair share of female attention wherever he went. He was widely considered the best drone pilot in the air force, a fact that Rosen had relayed to the president. However, what he had failed to mention in that discussion was that Daller had already indicated to his commanding officer that he was putting in his papers to leave the military and enter the private sector.

Cray entered the conference room wearing black military boots and a green air force flight suit, which was exactly how Daller was dressed, except that the flight suit issued to Cray by supply at Joint Base Andrews bore no rank or insignia. Therefore, when he introduced himself as a lieutenant colonel in the army, the look on the captain's face was one of confusion.

Cray began by asking the UAV pilot questions about himself and what gave him the greatest degree of satisfaction. Though he was normally not much of a talker, Daller sensed that he could trust the army officer in an air force flight suit and spent the next half hour talking about his personal life. When it came to the question of what made him happy, his answer was immediate: taking out terrorists and anyone else who tried to harm the United States.

Once Daller had finished answering the lieutenant colonel's questions, Cray reciprocated by giving his background. He followed with an explanation of Nemesis and its past missions.

"Is what you're doing legal?" asked Daller.

"We're an off-the-books team formed to bypass Washington bureaucracy and every level of government oversight. Therefore, what we're doing is not even remotely legal. We exist to protect the United States and China by whatever means we deem necessary. What that means is that we're not bringing anyone back for trial or sending them to Guantanamo. We resolve the situation ourselves. However, I understand your concern. Just realize that Nemesis doesn't act without orders from the commander-in-chief. Therefore, although the president's ass is hanging in the air, ours are covered. Do you have a problem with what I've said?"

"None. In fact, I couldn't agree more with this approach to keeping our country safe. Do you know how many times I've had to let some of the worst terrorists in the world get away because I couldn't get through the bureaucracy of the White House or Pentagon and get approval in time to launch my missiles? That's not counting the numerous occasions I aborted a strike because killing the bastard I'd tracked and identified would be politically offensive to a warlord, village leader, or someone of influence within the host country. I only wish you'd approached me sooner because I've reached my tipping point. I'm getting out."

"I hadn't heard," Cray said, surprised at this news.

"Drone pilots are leaving the military faster than replacement pilots can be trained. That means longer hours and fewer days off for everyone remaining in the program. I'm not married, so this doesn't especially bother me. But a lot of UAV pilots are, and their divorce rate is rapidly increasing. I love the military and my country. I especially love being a Sentinel pilot since the bad guys can't see my aircraft on radar. However, the air force doesn't seem to give the same weight to the skills and contributions of drone pilots as they do to those who fly manned aircraft. Therefore, we're the last to be promoted. I'm not bragging, but I'm the best drone pilot in the air force, and I got passed over for major below the zone. What does that tell you about my chances of getting to the rank of lieutenant colonel or colonel? The same could be said for my crew chief, Master Sergeant Peter Sherman."

"Let's pause for five minutes," Cray said as he got up from his chair and headed toward the door.

"Halfway down the hall to your right," Daller volunteered, assuming Cray needed a bathroom break.

Five minutes later, Cray returned. "Sorry about that. Where were we?"

"You were explaining why Nemesis needs drone capability and how I fit in."

"There's only ten of us in Nemesis, and you'd be the eleventh if you accept my offer. I can't promise that the hours, workload, or stress will be any less than here. In fact, they may even be greater. What I can promise is that we're extremely aggressive in dealing with our enemies, and our only interest is in protecting the homelands of the United States and China."

"Where would I be working?"

"You'd still be stationed at Creech, but your pilot station would be separated from the others so that no one could observe what you're doing. Your existing chain of command would be replaced by two people—me and the president. If anyone has an issue with anything you do or say, you don't argue with them. Instead, you tell them to call me. I work directly for the commander-in-chief. I promise any such discussions will be short."

They continued talking for another fifteen minutes, until they were interrupted by a knock on the door. Cray went to answer and took the envelope that was handed to him. In turn, he gave the envelope to Daller, who opened it with some trepidation, not knowing what he was being given.

"Congratulations, Major," Cray said as Daller looked in disbelief at his promotion order. "Your crew chief has also been promoted. If he elects to join us, he'll be the twelfth member of Nemesis. That's assuming you accept."

Daller looked Cray in the eye. "I'm ready for the challenge."

"Good answer."

"When do we get started?"

"We already have. How would you feel about taking out the leader of al-Qaeda?"

"Just tell me where he is."

"In a residence in Rasht, Tehran. Have you ever flown into Iran?"

From the surprised look on Daller's face, Cray knew the answer was no.

CHAPTER 19

THE MQ-170 SENTINEL that was now assigned to Nemesis, or more correctly to the White House's Statistical Analysis Division, wasn't stationed at Creech. Instead, it currently resided at a secret American airfield in Saudi Arabia's eastern desert, in an area referred to as Rub al Khali. This vast area stretched from central Saudi Arabia south to Yemen and east to the United Arab Emirates and Oman. The airfield was nothing to write home about, consisting of three clamshell-style hangars 150 feet long and 75 feet wide; three concrete runways, two of which could handle light aircraft, with the third constructed to land much heavier planes; four large cylindrical fuel tanks; and all the other lack of luxuries found on a secret military base in the middle of nowhere. Unfortunately, Rub al Khali was twelve hundred miles from Rasht, meaning that the Sentinel needed to be repositioned if it was to reach its target and return home with even a modicum of fuel. Therefore, Daller would have to hopscotch his drone from one secret airfield to another until the MQ-170 landed at the desert airfield outside the city of Halabjah, Iraq. A Kurdish stronghold on the Iranian border, the airfield was slightly less than 350 miles from Rasht and well within the combat range of the Sentinel.

Master Sergeant Pete Sherman was Daller's crew chief. They'd been a team for only six months, ever since the DOD received its first multiuse Sentinel. Sherman was five feet, ten inches tall, had brown eyes, and was as bald as a billiard ball, his hair having vanished half a decade earlier. A native of Cushing, Iowa, he had joined the air force twenty years ago at the age of eighteen, just after graduation from high school. He was neither fat nor thin and had the deep voice of a lifetime smoker, although he'd never smoked.

Sherman's day at the Rub al Khali airfield had begun innocently enough. He had finished his prep of the Sentinel for an upcoming mission and then released the MQ-170 to operations so that Daller could have control. He had just started turning off the last of his analytical equipment when the site commander walked into the hangar and handed him four manila envelopes, three of which carried the security classification of "Top Secret NOFORN," which meant that they couldn't be shown to a foreign national even if the person had the proper security clearance. The fourth envelope had only Sherman's name and rank printed on the front, which someone had apparently screwed up because his rank was listed as SMS, or senior master sergeant. He wished.

Opening the first classified envelope, he saw that he was being transferred, effective immediately, to the White House Statistical Analysis Division. Sherman had never heard of this division but assumed that since it was obviously connected to the White House, he hadn't previously had a need to know about its existence. The second envelope contained orders for him to board a C-130 Hercules transport that would taxi in front of his hangar shortly. He wasn't to worry about taking his personal items with him. They'd be packed and forwarded later. The Hercules would follow his MQ-170 aircraft as it hopscotched to its eventual destination—a desert airfield outside the city of Halabjah, Iraq. At each of the stops, he was to service the drone and get it back in the air as quickly as possible. The third classified order directed that upon his arrival in Halabjah, Sherman was to install within the internal bay of his Sentinel the contents of three crates that would be waiting for him in Iraq. Opening the fourth envelope, which was unclassified, he read that he'd been promoted to senior master sergeant, a promotion he'd believed had passed him by. He wanted to call Daller and ask what the hell was going on, but that idea was put on hold when the Sentinel started its engine in preparation for taxi, which meant that Daller was at the controls and couldn't take calls. Five minutes later, the C-130 landed, and Sherman boarded.

Sherman successfully supervised the Sentinel's refueling and maintenance as it made its way through Saudi Arabia and across Iraq. The C-130 then landed at the airfield outside Halabjah five minutes after the Sentinel. Once he had ensured that the drone was secured within the hangar where base ops had directed it be taken, and where three large wooden crates were waiting, Sherman uncrated the box marked "1," to which a pouch with a tamperproof strip was attached. Once he had removed the foam packing, his eyes went wide at the contents: Sherman was looking at what appeared to be an aircraft ordnance rack, and judging from the Cyrillic characters printed on the housing assembly, it was of Russian manufacture. The next two crates were just as eye-popping, each containing a five-hundred-pound dumb bomb. Both were fat and rounded and therefore decades old, lacking the sleeker aerodynamics of current bombs of this size.

Curious about what was expected of him, he tore off the tamperproof strip and removed the single piece of paper from within the opaque plastic pouch. His instructions consisted of just one sentence and two tasks: replace the Sentinel's internal ordnance rack with the one in the crate, and mate its electrical system to the drones so that the bombs could be released on command by the UAV pilot. That's when the last straw fell on the camel's back and he decided to call Daller on the secure line.

"What's going on, Captain?" Sherman asked in a stern voice before Daller had a chance to say a word. "I've just been reassigned to an organization that sounds like a bunch of number crunchers and politicians and flown to another garden spot in the desert, without so much as a change in clothes. Now they want me to mate two dumb bombs that belong in a museum to what looks like a Russian ordnance rack and put it into Darlene." Sherman had a habit of giving each of the drones he maintained a name because of the unique quirks in their electronic and mechanical systems.

"It's Major now, Senior Master Sergeant. We've both been promoted and transferred to the same organization. I'll tell you what I know about our new boss later, but for now you have to modify Darlene as quickly as possible before our target goes mobile."

"That's easier said than done since I don't have an operation manual, electrical diagram, or mechanical drawing of what I'm working on. I could end up shorting out the entire chassis by connecting two wires that were never intended to be mated. That's if I don't inadvertently release the two bombs."

"This sounds like a typical day for you, Pete."

"It's a typical SNAFU! Where's Darlene going?"

"Iran."

"Ballsy. Stupid, but ballsy."

Two hours before sunrise, Sherman looked like he'd been in a fight with a mountain lion. His shirt was torn from working in the tight confines of the Sentinel's internal bay, prodding, bending, and coercing two metal surfaces to physically and electronically attach. The installation had taken twelve hours and was ugly to the eye, something Rube Goldberg would have been proud of, but at 4:00 a.m. the two three-feet, four-inch-long Russian bombs were attached to a Russian ordnance rack in the belly of the Sentinel. Sherman would have loved to attach the bombs to a US ordnance rack, but none had the ability to hold this older type of bomb. In the end, however, it didn't matter. He was satisfied that they'd release from the MQ-170 on command, largely because he'd gutted the electronics system from the Russian rack and replaced it with an electronic harness from the Sentinel. He would later learn from Cray that the US had come into possession of the rack a year ago when the CIA hijacked a drone in flight by hacking into its computer system. The CIA had then steered the drone out of Russia and into Latvia, where an American military team was waiting to recover it. The two five-hundred-pound bombs had been obtained from a stockpile of Russian ordnance in a former Soviet bloc country.

Daller brought the Sentinel to life at 4:45 a.m. and, after a short taxi to the runway, took it airborne at 4:51 a.m. Cray's plan was to kill Zebari with a Russian-made bomb so that the Iranians would believe it was the Russians and not the Americans who had killed him. There would be ample reason to believe this because the al-Qaeda leader killed Russians in the Middle East with the same zeal that he killed Americans. To pin the attack on the Russians, one of the bombs had been disabled in a manner that made it appear to have malfunctioned. Therefore, when it was recovered, forensic experts would be able to examine the faulty bomb and determine it was of Russian manufacture. That was expedient for several reasons. If the Nemesis team or anyone else used an American weapon to kill Zebari, that would give Iran the moral high ground in the world of public opinion. It would also invite retaliation against American shipping in the Gulf. Last, the president also wanted to create a chasm of doubt as to how much Tehran could trust Moscow. Therefore, the recovered bomb would make it appear as if the Russians had assassinated Zebari.

At 8:47 a.m. the MQ-170 arrived at the coordinates that Daller had been given for the al-Qaeda leader's residence in Rasht. Daller went down his pre-launch checklist, which ended with him zooming the drone's powerful camera on the residence and adjusting his targeting computer. A second later, he released his weapons.

The blast radius for this five-hundred-pound bomb would be between one hundred and two hundred yards. For anyone standing twenty yards or less from the point of impact, there was a nearly zero chance of survival because the pressure from such a blast almost always caused lung hemorrhages, air bubbles in the circulatory system, and organ bruising and swelling. That didn't even consider the fragmentation of the bomb, which usually diced a body so that the other causes of death were moot.

After Daller opened the Sentinel's internal bay and released both weapons, the active five-hundred-pound bomb crashed through the roof of Zebari's house and exploded ten feet from him. One second he was sitting at the kitchen table, and the next his body didn't exist.

The second bomb released a split second after the first and went through a bedroom wall and into the large yard behind the house, destroying a storage shed along the way and eventually coming to rest twenty feet behind it. As planned, it never exploded.

The president of Iran was furious upon hearing that Zebari had been killed in an airstrike and that a foreign power had been arrogant enough to send a drone into his backyard and kill someone under his protection. He didn't care that the al-Qaeda leader was dead. In fact, his failure to detonate the dirty bomb in Washington necessitated his eventual demise to keep Iran's involvement a secret. What he cared about was how this act of aggression would affect the Supreme Leader's confidence in him as he approved the appointment of the country's president. If this intrusion went unanswered, it would be perceived as a sign of weakness and his approval would be rescinded, or he'd have a sudden health crisis and die unexpectedly.

Originally, he believed that only the Americans would be brazen enough to do this and would have the technology to evade his coastline detection system. Moreover, they had every reason to want Zebari dead given the casualties his followers had inflicted on the US military. That's why it was a surprise when his investigators reported that they'd found an unexploded five-hundred-pound bomb with Russian markings on it in the backyard of Zebari's residence. Forensics showed that the bomb was a twin of the one that had exploded within the house. That changed things and left two unanswered questions: had Zebari been secretly working for the Kremlin, or did he know something extremely important that the Russians wanted to keep secret? Either way, if Putin believed he could expand his power and influence within Iran's borders by blaming someone else for his act of aggression, he was mistaken, and the Iranian president vowed that Putin would soon discover the cost of that mistake.

CHAPTER 20

T HE CHANGZHENG 6 surfaced in the Bohai Sea, an inlet of the Yellow Sea on the northeast coast of China, and docked at the Lushun submarine base, which was a stone's throw from Dalian. Conti and Rotolo were resedated, placed in large canvas bags to hide them from prying eyes—especially those orbiting above the strategic naval facility—and taken to the Chou Shui Tze air base in the northwestern part of the city. There they were placed on a Shaanxi Y-8 medium-range transport aircraft and flown 1,251 miles to Mohe, the northernmost city in China.

When the plane landed, the two hooded prisoners were taken to the office of the prison commandant, Major Leung Tao, who had earlier received a call from President Liu mandating that the two men now standing before him be remanded to his facility for life and isolated from everyone except for himself and a select cadre of guards. Tao was familiar with this type of order because one of the other inmates, listed on the institution's manifest as prisoner number 41725, had arrived not long ago with the same set of instructions.

Major Leung stood in front of the shackled pair, who were standing between the two People's Liberation Army officers who had dragged them off the Shaanxi Y-8 aircraft. Astute at analyzing the type of people who occupied his prison and how much trouble they were going to give him, the major stared at the men for a full minute, looking at their facial expressions and body language. What he saw was a combination of suppressed arrogance, at least from Conti, bewilderment, and fear. Retreating to his desk, Leung picked up a two-foot-long bamboo baton and, with practiced motion, roughly jabbed the end of it into Conti's midsection and then Rotolo's, in rapid succession. Both men doubled over in pain and dropped to their knees before the PLA officers pulled them back onto their feet. This attention getter was the standard initiation for all who would spend the rest of their lives incarcerated within the prison.

"Welcome to Mohe," Leung said in broken English, "the most remote and secure military prison in China, which doesn't officially exist. You are now prisoners' number 41767 and 41768," he said, looking at each of the men in turn as he spoke their number. "If you identify yourself to anyone by anything other than this number, you will be severely beaten. You're here until you take your final breath. When you die, we'll dispose of you like trash and throw you in the furnace with the rest of the garbage. I know what you're thinking— that it's possible to escape from any prison, given enough time to analyze its weaknesses. Not Mohe. The nearest town is two hundred miles away. You'd starve to death or be eaten by wolves or bears long before you got there. The weather today is minus five degrees Fahrenheit, which is quite warm. In the dead of winter, you can expect it to get down to minus forty. Unfortunately, our antiquated boilers can only heat the interior of our prison to about fifty degrees Fahrenheit."

Conti and Rotolo looked increasingly haggard as Leung spoke, and their posture became stooped.

"You will be confined to your cell for all but one hour of the day unless you're taken away for interrogation, which will occur frequently. If you cooperate, these sessions will be less painful than if you try to resist. If you lie or try to hide information from us, you'll be traumatized and taken back to your cell, and the process will repeat until we're satisfied you've been truthful." Leung looked at Conti. "You," he said, grabbing him by the hair and pulling his face an inch from his, "I bet you're thinking that you can kill yourself. But we're experts at preventing suicide." He released Conti's hair. "You'll be allowed to shower and be given clean clothes once a week. If you're disruptive or disobey the guards, you'll be beaten, and your food will be taken away for one day. If you do that too often, you'll be force-fed and then beaten severely. Do you understand everything I've said?"

When both men nodded their understanding, the commandant smiled in satisfaction. "Excellent. Then let's begin our interrogation early so you won't miss dinner. The sergeant," Leung said, pointing to an unsmiling man at the back of the room, "will handle your initiation. And don't worry about your fingernails—they'll grow back."

It was 3:55 a.m., and Dante Acardi was crouched in the woods, intently looking through a pair of night-vision binoculars at the large one-story house in Caprarola, one hundred yards away. Beside him were fifteen officers from the Polizia di Stato's elite tactical unit. All were riding out the last five minutes until "E-Hour," the official time they would launch their assault on Conti's safehouse, which had been discovered thanks to Montanari's initial hacking of the terrorist's computer.

There were no flares or yells to signal the start of the assault. All members of the tactical unit had their watches synced, and at exactly 4:00 a.m. they broke from their hiding places in the woods and initiated a planned series of actions. While five men secured the exterior of the property, the remaining ten prepared to enter through the front door, the only way into the house. From this group, one man placed a breaching charge on the front door and gave notice through his mic that the breach was imminent. Three seconds after he pressed the timer on the explosive charge, the front door was reduced to splinters. Immediately thereafter, another officer came forward and hurled two stun grenades, also known as flashbangs, into the far reaches of the residence, one on either side of the house. Each explosive device produced a seven-million-candela flash of light that momentarily activated the photoreceptor cells in the eyes of anyone exposed, causing blindness that lasted approximately five seconds. The flashbang also produced a 170-decibel bang, which not only deafened victims but also disturbed the fluid in their ears, causing a loss of balance.

Once the flashbangs had exploded, the ten officers entered the residence and spread out. As this was happening, the four al-Qaeda fighters inside jumped out of their beds and grabbed their guns. Disoriented, they stumbled out of their rooms and fired their AK-74s at the ceiling, the floor, and other directions that didn't matter because of the disconnect between their brain and muscles. The tactical unit didn't have that lack of muscular coordination, and the four terrorists went down in a hail of return gunfire.

Once the residence was secured, Acardi entered and directed the search of the premises, although the group's armament cache wasn't hard to find since crates of weapons and explosives filled four rooms and were stacked from floor to ceiling.

It took an eighteen-wheeler to transport all the crates to an Italian army base. Unfortunately, an inspection of the crates by explosive ordnance disposal revealed that every serial number and other indicator of origin had been mechanically removed or chemically erased from the crates' contents.

Nevertheless, the origin of the weapons and explosives was eventually determined thanks to information provided by both Conti and Rotolo. Conti gave up his suppliers in the first hour of his interrogation, after three of his fingernails were ripped off. He told his interrogator everything else he knew, including the role that Haamid Khakwani had played in the operation, when the remaining two fingernails on his left hand suffered the same fate. Since the sergeant responsible for extracting information believed a prisoner would do anything to stop the pain, he verified what Conti had told him with information extracted from Rotolo. The latter prisoner was able to tolerate a great deal more pain than his boss and lasted through the extraction of all ten fingernails and two of his toenails before he verified what Conti had said.

The Sentinel drone's pilot was patient, following the stooped elderly man as he shuffled from the Pakistan Academy of Sciences to his residence. The house, which could more accurately be described as a hovel—crudely constructed of derelict pieces of wood, with a blue tarp covering a third of its roof—was in the crosshairs of Major Adam Daller's weapons system. Adjusting the MQ-170's flight path and angle of attack to minimize collateral damage to the structures adjoining the residence, he turned the drone fifty degrees to starboard, dipped its nose two degrees below the horizon, and opened the doors to its internal weapons bay, which Sherman had returned to its original configuration. Attached to the ordnance rack were two Hellfire II AGM-114 missiles, each of which had a kill radius of fifty feet.

Daller released one missile, and once it was clear of the aircraft, its engine ignited. Generating 10 g's of initial thrust, it quickly accelerated to 950 miles an hour and maintained that speed as it pierced the blue tarp over Khakwani's hovel and impacted the ground two feet from where he was standing. The al-Qaeda scientist never heard the explosion. Instead his sensory perceptions ended with the intensely bright light that blinded him and the momentary sensation of intense heat as his body dissipated in a maelstrom of fire.

An hour later, the president of Pakistan was briefed on the attack. There was no doubt in his mind that the explosive device had come from an American drone or piloted aircraft. Very few countries had the stealth technology to penetrate his country's air defenses and deliver such a surgical strike, and only one had previously exercised that capability, in its attack on Osama bin Laden.

He knew that President Ballinger had a hard-on for terrorists and didn't much care about borders when going after them—not that he didn't have good reason for killing Haamid Khakwani, since he was one of many within this country who actively supported and encouraged terrorism against the West. Nevertheless, the Pakistani president was angry, not because his country's sovereignty had been violated or because of an insignificant scientist's death, but because this would force him to at least verbally confront the most lethal military and economic superpower in the world. If he didn't respond to this aggression, he'd appear to his people as an impotent head of state, which was exactly what he was when trying to stand toe-to-toe with the United States. Since a military reprisal against this superpower was out of the question, his only option was to summon the US ambassador to Pakistan to the presidential palace and read him the riot act.

Two hours after he'd been summoned, the American ambassador arrived. He appeared outwardly calm as the Pakistani president verbally eviscerated him for a full ten minutes in front of a hastily assembled audience of government officials, advisors, and members of the press. Following the tirade, all of which had been televised, the ambassador calmly reached into the breast pocket of his jacket, removed a folded letter-size piece of paper, and handed it to the Pakistani president.

Not knowing what it contained and seeking to maintain his bravado for the audience, the Pakistani leader took and read the communique from President Ballinger in full view of the audience. The message was extremely blunt and to the point: either act against militant groups and individuals who wanted to harm the United States or else the US military would identify, target, and eliminate them on its own. After reading the communique, the president of Pakistan abruptly asked the ambassador to follow him to an adjoining conference room, while those in the large room watched their departure in stunned silence.

"If I make this communique public," the president said in passable English, "the United States will be looked upon as a bully and tyrant. We're a sovereign country—you politely ask for our help; you don't demand it or threaten us."

The ambassador, in what was obviously a preplanned action, hit a speed-dial number on his cell phone and handed it to the head of state. A moment later, President Ballinger answered.

After initial greetings, the president of Pakistan repeated the threat that he'd made to the ambassador.

"Show the damn communique to whoever you want," said Ballinger. "You harbored Osama bin Laden, currently hide Awalmir Afridi, and leak the intelligence we provide you to our enemies. I intend to eliminate, with or without your help, some very bad people who reside in your country and want to harm the United States."

"You don't understand the history of my country or the many diverse groups that occupy our land. It's a complicated dynamic. We're also a sovereign country, not a territory of the United States. The United Nations will condemn your actions, as will your media. We'll do as we please."

"I couldn't care less what the UN thinks. They haven't voted in favor of anything the US has endorsed for as long as I've been in office. As for the media, they have as much credibility as Congress, which is to say close to zero. Let me be clear: I'll no longer let Pakistan be a training ground and safe harbor for those who would destroy our way of life. End this threat to the United States, or I will."

The USS *Vermont*, a Virginia-class nuclear attack submarine, was sixty feet below the choppy surface of the Adriatic Sea when it locked on its prey. The 370-foot-long hunter-killer submarine, which had a beam of thirty-four feet and a draft of thirty-two feet, carried both MK-48 torpedoes and Tomahawk cruise missiles. As the captain looked at the real-time images of the Panamanian-flagged merchant vessel on his console screen, a tracking solution was automatically calculated and fed into the torpedo's guidance system. Once this occurred, he ordered firing point procedures and, after reaffirming the readiness of the weapon, gave the command to shoot. The crewman who received this order immediately pressed a button that sent an electronic command to the torpedo tube's air flask, which dumped air into a piston ram. This pressure, which was higher than the outside sea pressure, forced the torpedo out of the tube and away from the submarine. All this occurred in not more than the blink of an eye.

Once the torpedo was free, the weapon's engine engaged. The internal guidance system then took over. Cutting through the water at over twenty-eight knots, the 3,520-pound torpedo locked onto its lumbering target, and less than a minute later, a high-explosive charge of 650 pounds impacted the merchant vessel's hull amidships.

The *Capira* was literally blown in two, with both sections of the ship staying afloat for only seconds before sinking straight to the bottom. At this point the captain of the *Vermont* sent a message to Secretary of Defense Rosen, confirming the sinking of the ship that, according to intelligence, had belonged to the Iranian military and had been responsible for transporting the dirty bomb to Washington.

Dante Acardi understood the risks of being a law enforcement officer. Every person who wore a shield knew that when they left home to report for duty, they might never return. What he couldn't understand, however, was treachery among those who were sworn to uphold the law. That kind of behavior made him, and every other police officer he knew, furious. He carried that pent-up rage within him as he walked around the palatial living room of Niccolo Pecora, the Taranto judge who had ordered the arrest of Bruno, Donati, and Donais. Acardi had no doubt that the jurist was on Conti's payroll, because the fifty-year-old came from a modest background, with a father who worked as a shoemaker and a mother who worked as a seamstress. In other words, he had been dirt poor when he became a judge but now lived in a ten-thousand-square-foot residence on a fifty-acre estate. Acardi's loathing for the judge grew as he took in the luxurious trappings around him, which he viewed as an arrogant manifestation of betrayal. Because of this man's treachery, his nephew was dead. He realized that was a slight bastardization of the truth, but it was close enough.

Acardi looked at the judge, whom he'd gagged and tied to a heavy brown leather club chair, with disdain. The jurist was squirming and trying to say something, although the gag prevented anything intelligible from being heard. Anyway, Acardi wasn't interested. Looking at his watch, he saw that he needed to get moving if he was going to make his return flight to Rome. Taking one last look around the room, which he'd earlier drenched in gasoline, he pulled a lighter from his pocket and lit a piece of paper he had taken off a nearby desk.

Pecora, who clearly understood what was about to happen, frantically tried to tip over the chair and get out of his bonds, but the chair was far too heavy and wide to tip over, and the bonds too tight to break or pull apart. With the flame nearly at his fingertips, Acardi dropped the scrap of paper on the floor and dashed toward the door leading outside. Turning around for one last look, he saw that the corrupt judge was surrounded by flames and would soon be immolated.

Acardi took a deep breath and shook his head slightly. "I've changed my mind," he said, recognizing that he'd just made a spur-of-the-moment decision.

Pecora's facial expression resonated with hope, as if Acardi had thrown him a life preserver. That changed a second later, when he apparently saw the look in Acardi's eye.

"This fire won't give me closure. I sent my nephew into harm's way. Therefore, I need to be the one who avenges his death," Acardi said. "Oculum pro oculo, as the Bible says." With that he drew the gun from his shoulder holster and put a bullet in the center of Pecora's forehead.

Three months after Judge Niccolo Pecora was killed by the mafia for refusing to accept a bribe—at least according to the report issued by Deputy Commissioner Dante Acardi— Mauro Bruno was sitting at his desk, which was to say the office conference table, opening the mail. Most of the items in front of him were advertisements, which he quickly discarded. That dwindled the pile down to two letters, both addressed to him. One was from Dante Acardi, who, true to his word, had referred another potential client to the fledgling firm, his third referral in as many months. The second was a plain white envelope that had no return address, only a Venice postmark over the stamp.

Opening the envelope, Bruno saw that it contained a single piece of heavy linen stationery, which seemed odd given the cheapness of the envelope. The stationery seemed strangely familiar to him, although he couldn't put his finger on why. When he unfolded the page, that question was quickly answered—the letter had been written by him on March 23, 1996, the day his late wife Katarina, a municipal police officer in Venice who was pregnant with their first child, had been killed while on night duty. The murders, from which he had been forced to recuse himself because of his obvious personal involvement, had never been solved.

He now held in his hand the love letter that he'd handed his wife as she left their residence that day, but which hadn't been found on her body when it was discovered. Two emotions that had receded over time instantly returned—intense anger and a resolute desire for revenge. Stuck to the bottom of the letter was a yellow Post-it note. Written in black ink with a heavy hand was an email address and, below that, a message: "I know who killed your wife and unborn child."

AUTHOR'S NOTES

This is a work of fiction, and the characters within are likewise fictional and are not meant to represent any person or company in the real world.

The author got the idea for this Bruno-Donati-Donais novel while reading an article on the Italian government's plans to allow offshore oil and gas drilling in the Adriatic Sea—one of the most pristine areas on the Italian peninsula. Monopoli is a wonderful town on the Adriatic side of the heel of Italy, which is frequently referred to as the Apulia region. Going there is like walking back in time. Founded by the Greeks, Monopoli is different from many towns in the area in that it's not a destination for those looking to stay at a beach resort. Instead, it retains its centuries-old fishing tradition, which one can see from looking at the numerous traditional fishing boats tied up in port near fishermen mending their nets. As noted, the town is thirty-seven miles from the Bari Karol Wojtyła Airport, which does offer an EasyJet flight from Milan. The Hotel Vecchio Mulino exists and is essentially as described, although liberties were taken with the descriptions of the lounge and lobby. In addition, the coroner's building and office, its staff, and its distance from the hotel were changed for the sake of the story line. Taranto is, as represented, forty miles from Monopoli and is also in the Apulia region, but on the Ionian Sea side of the heel.

In researching what the government pays Italy's minister of justice, the author was surprised to learn that Italy, a country $2.6 trillion in debt, pays its average lawmakers between $20,700 and $26,000 a month, which includes perks and expenses—more than lawmakers in any other EU country. According to Barbie Latza Nadeau of *The Daily Beast*,

> Italian lawmakers travel free by air, rail, road, and sea within Italy, yet they can still file for up to $1,700 in receipt-free travel expenses as part of their monthly earnings. They are each given a tax-free housing allowance to live in Rome—even if they already own private houses in the capital. They are also allowed $5,000 every month in secretarial and research support costs on top of their salaries, even if they use the parliamentary staff or choose not to employ their own staff. They enjoy subsidized dining in a gourmet cafeteria where they eat T-bone steaks and grilled swordfish for just a few dollars per plate, not to mention enjoying the services of hairdressers, barbers, and manicurists.

Lawmakers in Italy do quite well.

The statement that the northern Ionian Sea has a higher concentration of microplastics than the Adriatic Sea is accurate. Microplastics present a threat to marine ecosystems in the area and are found in 46.25 percent of mussels and 47.2 percent of three species of fish in the northern Ionian Sea.

The author based the interior and exterior of the apartment where BD&D Investigations is located on an actual 2,800-square-foot apartment that rents for $6,700 per month in the Corso Di Porta Romana neighborhood of Milan. The author decided to put BD&D Investigations there not only because it was upscale and presented a good image for the firm, which Donati probably would have insisted on, but also because it provided a nice place for Donais to live and work while not at her Paris residence.

The description of the symbol found by Donais on the artifact is accurate, and the symbol is used by al-Qaeda in Iraq. The open book above the globe represents the Quran. The flag emerging from the Quran indicates al-Qaeda's goal of creating an Islamic caliphate, and the rifle and fist represent its militancy. These symbols' emergence from the Quran indicates that the holy book is the foundation of al-Qaeda's mission in Islam and communicates the group's intent to establish an Islamic state that includes both Lebanon and Israel. The globe symbolizes that the group's goals are worldwide.

The description of a dirty bomb is accurate. Such a bomb isn't a nuclear weapon. Instead, it is radiological material paired with a conventional explosive. The purpose of the weapon is not to cause massive loss of life, but to disperse radioactive material throughout the blast-wave radius to cause panic, psychological trauma, and economic damage. It is therefore not considered a weapon of mass destruction. Instead, some refer to it as a weapon of mass disruption. Decontamination of the thousands of victims and cleanup of an affected area would require considerable time and expense.

My apologies to Tumi for the use of the Latitude suitcase to house the dirty bomb. The author chose it because of its sturdiness and the fact that Tumi is an internationally recognized brand that wouldn't cause as much suspicion as one manufactured in Iran or another Middle Eastern country.

The *Capira* is a fictional ship, although another ship by that name, and with the same physical dimensions, was built in Seattle in 1920 and sunk by a German submarine in 1942.

The information regarding diplomatic pouches is accurate. A diplomatic pouch is defined as any properly identified and sealed package, pouch, envelope, bag, or other container that is used to transport official correspondence, documents, and other articles intended for official use. The exterior markings must indicate "Diplomatic Pouch" in English and bear the seal of the sending entity. In addition, Article 27.3 of the Vienna Convention on Diplomatic Relations indicates that properly designated diplomatic pouches "shall not be opened or detained." Although inspection of a pouch by x-ray would not physically break the external seal of the shipment, such an action is interpreted as the modern-day electronic equivalent of "opening" a pouch. For a deeper dive into diplomatic pouches, please go to https://www.state.gov/ofm/customs/c37011.htm.

The oil and gas platform described in this novel is a generic hybrid assembled to facilitate the story line. The number of crew members on a platform varies with the size of the rig, with some of the larger platforms accommodating as many as two hundred workers. Although the work schedule is not the same for every rig, most companies have crew members work two weeks and then give them two weeks off. If a person occupies a skilled position, he or she is usually given three weeks off. A standard workday is considered to be twelve hours. The average pay per employee varies by position, employer, and geographic location. The reference source used for this novel noted the median pay per worker as $93,000 per year. However, petroleum engineers may earn $135,000, and geophysicists $125,000, whereas service unit operators are paid an annual wage of $64,000. The number of workers domiciled per room on a rig varies. Employees in senior positions are authorized private rooms, whereas a person at the low end of the totem pole may have three to seven roommates. As represented, alcohol and nonprescription drugs are prohibited, and being caught with either will result in an employee's immediate termination. Smoking is also prohibited on oil and gas platforms, except in designated areas where those who require a nicotine fix can light up. Matches are provided in these areas and are prohibited on the rest of the platform.

The *Trochus* is a fictional ship and a composite of LNG carriers. As written, liquefied natural gas is predominately methane, with some ethane in the mix. When being transferred to a ship, the gas goes through a cooling process and is brought down to a temperature of minus 260 degrees Fahrenheit, converting it to a liquid, which is 1/600th the volume of natural gas in a gaseous state.

The author toyed with locating the NATO summit closer to Civitavecchia and blowing up the *Trochus* when research showed that exploding an LNG carrier ship could be as destructive as detonating several nuclear bombs. However, that story line went into the trash can when the author discovered that an LNG ship is considered safer than one used for crude oil—reflected by the fact that insurance rates are 25 percent cheaper for LNG carriers than those transporting oil. There are numerous reasons for this difference. For one, liquid methane doesn't burn; only the vapors are flammable. In addition, LNG tanks are all double-walled and very thick, making them difficult to penetrate.

Once LNG is converted to a gaseous state, it will burn only if the air-to-fuel proportions are between 5 and 15 percent—a narrow range. Igniting it is also problematic. Whereas the auto-ignition temperature of gasoline is 495 degrees Fahrenheit, and diesel 600 degrees, methane doesn't ignite until 1,004 degrees. Therefore, it takes more than a hot surface to provide the ignition impetus for natural gas.

Next! Still liking the idea of a gas explosion, the author decided to use another method to ignite the natural gas. I mean, if Mark Wahlberg can do it in *Shooter*, how hard could it be? As it turned out, because of the aforementioned specific air-fuel ratio and temperature requirements, it wasn't all that easy to formulate a plausible way to transmit gas several blocks through a sewer line and then ignite it on demand. I thought of one possible solution and was quite proud of it when I mentioned it at dinner to a good friend of mine, Dr. Charles Pappas, one of the smartest people I have ever met. The former practicing surgeon indicated that I needed to rethink the ignition process because the contemplated trigger mechanism had an insufficient amount of power to realistically work. My idea was DOA. Thankfully, Dr. Pappas did offer an intriguing solution. The author gladly accepted and purloined the suggestion thereby coming up with a plausible way to ignite the natural gas.

The Tre Taverne in Taranto is fictional, but a tavern by that name, the Three Taverns, did exist in the third century BC on the ancient Appian Way. Thirty miles from Rome, it was designed as a rest and reception area for travelers.

THE ARTIFACT

The Pakistan Academy of Sciences exists and has the role of scientific advisor to the Pakistani government. However, there is no evidence, at least from this author's research, that anyone presently or previously associated with this institution has ever been involved with acts of terror. For the sake of the story line, the author needed someone who had the scientific knowledge to construct what amounted to a detonator for the LNG that was released into the sewer lines. That person also needed to be a top-notch scientist and have an extreme hatred for the West. Therefore, Haamid Khakwani was created to satisfy both needs.

As written, al-Qaeda is a militant Sunni Islamist organization. It was founded in 1988 by Osama bin Laden, Abdullah Azzam, and several others during the Soviet invasion of Afghanistan. In contrast, 90 percent of Iranians are Shia, and the other 10 percent Sunni.

The description of the Quirinal Palace, minus the representation of its subterranean areas and security, is accurate. The palace is 1,110,500 square feet, making it the ninth-largest palace in the world. By comparison, the White House is one-twentieth its size. The Quirinal is the official residence of the president of Italy and was built on the highest of the seven hills of Rome. It was completed in 1583 and has served as the residence for thirty popes, four kings of Italy, and twelve presidents of the Italian Republic.

Civitavecchia is approximately fifty miles from Rome and does not have an LNG terminal, which was placed there for the sake of the story line because the author needed an LNG facility relatively near the Quirinal. There are only three LNG terminals in Italy: the Adriatic LNG terminal near Rovigo, the Panigaglia LNG terminal near La Spezia, and the Toscana LNG terminal near Livorno.

The one-time pad (OTP) is accurately described by Donais. It is a mathematically unbreakable type of encryption. The Soviet Union, as written, changed its communications to one-time pads in 1948 and crippled the NSA's signal intelligence efforts for years—an event the NSA refers to as Black Friday.

The basic story of the refugees on the dinghy from Sabratha, Libya, is accurate, and as many as 170 refugees are known to have been placed on similar dinghies from this location. This often results in drownings, suffocations, hypothermia, and starvation. Sometimes refugees are initially placed on a boat and then, once at sea, are forced into a dinghy so crowded they can hardly move. Smugglers have found this to be an efficient way to transport refugees without the danger of having their boats confiscated at sea in the event they're intercepted by a naval or police vessel. This is a treacherous journey. In the first four months of 2017, for example, more than a thousand people died going from Libya to Italy. The fuel provided is only enough to reach international waters, where the smugglers, who are usually paid between $750 and $3,500 per person, tell those aboard they'll be picked up by the Italians and brought to shore. Sabratha, Libya, is a frequent departure point for refugees' journey to Italy.

The Agency for External Information and Security, known as AISE, and the Agency for Internal Information and Security, known as AISI, exist and are the Italian equivalent of, respectively, the CIA and FBI.

The Ospedale San Giacomo in Monopoli exists and appears to be a top-of-the-line medical facility. However, liberties were taken as to the services it provides, the helipad, the emergency room, and just about everything else associated with the hospital but the name. The author needed a hospital in Monopoli and therefore chose this medical facility.

The aircraft and transports used for the British prime minister and the chancellor of Germany are accurately described. The description of the presidential motorcade that is flown in by US Air Force C-17 aircraft is accurate. An excellent description of the anatomy of a US presidential motorcade can be found at http://www.thedrive.com/the-war-zone/4518/the-fascinating-anatomy-of-the-presidential-motorcade.

The description of the electronic countermeasures Suburban is accurate, at least from what the author has been able to obtain from publicly available information. Recently, the author observed a presidential motorcade traveling down a street near his residence in southwest Florida. Although the motorcycles, Suburbans, two presidential limousines, and a plethora of other security vehicles flew past at about sixty miles per hour, the electronic countermeasures Suburban was impossible to miss since it had a virtual antenna farm on its roof.

The Land Phalanx Weapon System, or LPWS, is accurately described and is the shore variant of the Phalanx CIWS ("sea-whiz") system deployed on nearly every class of US Navy combat ship.

The Mark XII IFF System, as described, is a cooperative question-and-answer identification system that enables military and civilian controllers to identify aircraft, vehicles, or forces as friendly, neutral, or hostile. In addition, it determines their bearing and range.

The Hotel Hassler, Westin Excelsior, and St. Regis are all spectacular hotels in Rome. If you have an opportunity to stay at the Hassler, take it. The descriptions of the hotel's location, its penthouses, and the presidential suite are accurate.

Italy's minister of economic development is, as represented, responsible for recommending economic policies, telecommunications, energy and mineral resources, consumer protection, tourism, and business incentives. If there's a problem with public services within Italy, he usually gets blamed.

Italy's ministers of justice, past and present, have been and are honorable public servants. As mentioned, characters used in this novel are fictional and are not meant to depict real-world individuals.

The mission of the NATO Defense College and its location are accurately depicted. However, for the sake of the story line, a dorm was placed within the confines of the college even though the author's research could not determine whether there is a residence within the NDC for those who attend the college. The author needed that assumption to cement what Zebari would gain by blowing up the campus at night.

The information that Antonio Conti provided Bruno and Donati regarding the rig's kitchen was purloined from a Q & A paper given to the author by urologist extraordinaire Dr. Meir Daller, titled "How to Lose Stubborn Belly Fat: The Dr. Daller Way." It's a remarkable work. However, the author will confess that he's still a work in progress in adhering to both the letter and the spirit of the paper and that he occasionally confuses a cheeseburger, french fries, and pizza with whole foods.

In many respects, the author imparts his personality, likes, dislikes, prejudices, and so forth to his characters. That is certainly the case with Indro Montanari's love of spaghetti sauce and cannoli. During the author's youth, with Sicilian grandparents, there always seemed to be a pot of spaghetti sauce on the stove and a box of cannoli in the refrigerator.

During the author's travels to Italy, he sampled cannoli from nearly one hundred pastry shops throughout Italy and discovered the nearest thing to his grandmother's cannoli at the Laboratorio Pasticceria Roberto in Taormina, Sicily.

BleachBit, used by Conti to wipe his computer memory, is as described and was apparently used by Hillary Clinton. In fact, her photo can be found on the company's website: https://www.bleachbit.org/.

The description of the F740 Combat Rubber Raiding Craft, or CRRC, is accurate. Commonly used by special forces, these vessels can be transported by aircraft or submarine and inflated by foot or with the use of a CO_2 tank. And since they have multiple chambers, they can continue to operate even if punctured by bullets. A CRRC can hold up to ten people.

The electromagnetic personnel interdiction control, or EPIC weapon, is as described. This portable weapon was developed by the US Navy and emits an electromagnetic pulse (EMP) that temporarily scrambles the nerve endings in a person's inner ear, causing nausea and affecting one's sense of balance, although it causes no permanent damage to the body. EMP waves can penetrate walls as easily as a hot knife cuts through butter. For the sake of the story line, the author assumed the EPIC used by the characters had a standalone power supply.

Mohe is the northernmost town in China, and only a river separates it from Siberia. The author, who resides in Florida, was there in February, wearing every piece of cashmere that he owned since it was minus twenty-six degrees Fahrenheit when he arrived, even without the wind. The black prison in Mohe may or may not exist. However, if you drive from the airport to the city, you'll see a structure halfway there and to your left that resembles a prison. Although it's in the distance, you can see watchtowers and high walls topped with razor wire.

The submarine Changzheng 6 exists. Whether it has ever been in the Mediterranean is unknown. However, it was a convenient way for the author to transport Conti and Rotolo to China. Military abbreviations are often confusing. "SSBN," which describes the Changzheng 6, denotes a submarine (SS) that carries ballistic missiles (B) and is nuclear-powered (N).

The Lockheed Martin RQ-170 Sentinel flying wing drone is a stealth unmanned aerial vehicle (UAV) operated by the 432nd Operations Group wing of the USAF's Air Combat Command at Creech Air Force Base, Nevada. In the language of military designations for aircraft other than an airplane, "R" designates reconnaissance, "Q" refers to an unmanned aerial vehicle, and "M" is for a multimission aircraft. With a wingspan of sixty-six feet and a body length of slightly less than fifteen feet, the four-and-a-half-ton RQ-170 is thought to have an operational ceiling of fifty thousand feet. However, there is no MQ-170 drone, which was created for the sake of the story line. Only the RQ-170 exists. The author needed a stealth drone with weapons capability to penetrate Iranian airspace and therefore created a variant of the Sentinel for that purpose.

Creech Air Force Base, Nevada, is the military's command and control facility for remotely piloted aircraft systems. Its pilots engage in daily overseas contingency operations of UAVs across the globe. In addition to the Sentinel, the airmen at Creech fly the MQ-1B Predator and its successor, the MQ-9 Reaper drone. The base is located fifty-four miles from Groom Lake AFB, which is also known as Area 51.

Daller's comments on the complaints of drone pilots are accurate. Drone pilots generally work twelve to fourteen hours a day, six days a week. That equates to about eighteen hundred hours a year at the controls of a drone. This leads to stress, fatigue, war weariness, and general wear and tear on the pilot. In comparison, it's about six times the three-hundred-hour annual cap for other air force pilots. As a result, it is estimated that up to a quarter of the air force pilots trained and authorized to fly drones quit their jobs each year. A strong draw for those leaving the military is the fact that a private-sector drone pilot makes, on average, four times as much as a military UAV pilot. Discontent also stems from the fact that drone pilots are sometimes viewed as "second tier" airmen, meaning they don't garner the same respect as pilots of manned aircraft. This perception is reflected in the unequal promotion of drone and manned aircraft airmen. Regarding the novel's mention of Washington bureaucracy, according to former UAV pilot Bruce Black, he and his team watched Abu Musab al-Zarqawi, the founder of al-Qaeda in Iraq, for six hundred hours before he was eventually killed by a bomb from a manned aircraft.

The once-secret desert base at Rub al Khali exists. Its description is accurate and was taken from an article by Noah Shachtman that appeared in *Wired*. Further details can be found by going to https://www.wired.com/2013/02/secret-drone-base-2/.

The secret desert airfield outside Halabjah, Iraq, does not exist, at least to the author's knowledge. Situated on the Iraq-Iran border, this fictional airfield allowed the author to exploit this desert area for the sake of the story line and permitted Daller to place the Sentinel close to Rasht.

The description of stealth aircraft and technologies is accurate. A good article if one wants to delve further into this area is available on the website Defence Aviation: https://

www.defenceaviation.com/2016/05/how-to-detect-stealth-aircraft.html.

The Lushun submarine base and the Chou Shui Tze air base are accurately represented. Lushun is strategically located between the Bohai Strait and the Miaodao and Penglai Cape of Shandong Province. Because of this, it's considered the "door to Beijing and Tianjin" and is responsible for protecting both cities. The author has been to Dalian numerous times. Located twenty miles from Lushun, it's a very beautiful city with some of the best seafood in mainland China.

The technical information on the Hellfire II missile, or AGM-114, is accurate. Weighing a little more than a hundred pounds, it has a kill radius of fifty feet and a wounding radius of sixty-five feet. There are many types of Hellfire missiles, and they vary in cost from $25,000 to $99,000. The one used against Haamid Khakwani had a blast fragmentation/ incendiary warhead. With a range of a little over 8,700 yards, it is normally used against bunkers, light vehicles, urban targets, and caves.

The description of the stun grenade, or flashbang, is accurate. It does produce a blinding flash of light. With an intensity of about seven million candelas, it will blind someone for approximately five seconds. It also emanates a 170-decibel bang that will not only temporarily deafen victims but also cause them to lose their balance.

The USS *Vermont*, SBN-792, is a Virginia-class submarine and is accurately described. Interestingly, this new class of submarine has a photonics mast that has replaced the traditional periscope. Rising like a car antenna in a telescopic motion from the sail or fin of a submarine, the mast provides imaging, navigation, electronic warfare, and communications functions to various consoles within the vessel.

It should be noted that a torpedo is launched with the command "shoot" and not "fire." Fire on a submarine means exactly that—flames, things burning, smoke, and so on. The procedures for shooting a torpedo were taken from several articles the author read and therefore may not be as exact a description as one would get from an old salt, but the data is nevertheless viewed as extremely accurate by someone who is former air force!

ACKNOWLEDGMENTS

An author is often a user. For this author that has certainly been the case, as I have continued to rely on an extraordinary group of friends, who patiently provided their technical expertise and opinions on this novel's story line. Because an author has a fragile ego and constantly lives in a state of denial, sometimes their comments scarred this ego. Other times, however, stitches or even an occasional emergency surgery was required. Still, these cuts, bruises, scrapes, and sometime lacerations of the arteries eventually healed.

Thank you to Kerry Refkin for another great edit of the manuscript and for insights into what drives a character's behavior. You're a genius.

Thank you to the group—Scott Cray, Dr. Charles and Aprille Pappas, Dr. John and Cindy Cancelliere, Doug Ballinger, Alexandra Parra, Ed Houck, Cheryl Rinell, Mark Iwinski, Mike Calbot, and Dr. Meir Daller—for continuing to be my sounding boards.

My thanks to Zhang Jingjie for her research. Again, no one is better at finding that needle in the haystack.

Thanks to Dr. Kevin Hunter and Rob Durst for technology advice and their computer and cybersecurity skills.

To Clay Parker, Jim Bonaquist, and Greg Urbancic: thank you for the extraordinary legal advice you continue to provide.

To Bill Wiltshire and Debbie Layport: thanks again for your superb financial and accounting skills.

To our friends Zoran Avramoski, Piotr Cretu, Neti Gaxholli, Aleksandar Toporovski, and Billy DeArmond: thanks for your insights.

Thank you to Doug and Winnie Ballinger and Scott and Betty Cray, who continue to help so many people who believed that hopelessness was their norm—until you came along! Well done.

ABOUT THE AUTHOR

Alan Refkin is the author of five previous works of fiction and the coauthor of four business books on China. He received the Editor's Choice Award for *The Wild Wild East* and for *Piercing the Great Wall of Corporate China*, for which he also received the Rising Star Award. The author and his wife, Kerry, live in southwest Florida, where he is currently working on his next Bruno-Donati-Donais novel. More information on the author, including his blog, can be obtained at alanrefkin.com.

Printed in the United States
By Bookmasters